NO MAN'S ISLAND

BY JESSICA MANN

Fiction

Nonfiction

Jessica Mann

NO MAN'S ISLAND

PUBLISHED FOR THE CRIME CLUB
BY
Doubleday & Company, Inc.
Garden City, New York
1983

All of the characters in this book are fictitious,
and any resemblance to actual persons,
living or dead,
is purely coincidental.

Library of Congress Cataloging in Publication Data

Mann, Jessica.
No Man's Island.

I. Title.
PR6063.A374N6 1983 823'.914
ISBN 0-385-18907-9
Library of Congress Catalog Card Number: 83-45002

First Edition in the United States of America

NO MAN'S ISLAND

WHEN THE EXPLOSION CAME, the girl's neck cracked straight across. Tamara Hoyland, who had been expecting it for minutes, was under the table with her unspilled drink still in her hand by the time the fragments of glass from the pub mirror finished falling beside her. Sherds of blue from the girl's dress, of yellow from her flowing hair, and green from the water-lilies tinkled to the floor. The mirror had been ninety years old. Nothing else in the Rose and Crown's saloon bar actually broke, except for some glasses stacked beside the sink, but the whole building seemed to rock. The publican said, "It's like the bloody blitz."

The only other customer went to the door and admitted a cloud of dust and rain.

"The whole terrace is going," he said.

"That'll save the bulldozers a job."

The street had been cleared for redevelopment, and in the last few weeks even the squatters had left for better accommodation. Mike, Rory, and Tamara had shared their rooms with spiders and rodents.

Tamara had left Mike and Rory in what they called their pad. The men were disentangling sticky tape, their backs to Tamara, while she made her adjustments to the timing device. When they turned round, she was crouched on the mattress again, looking martyred.

"Worse?" Mike asked with some sympathy. But Rory was irritated.

"You ought to get that stomach of yours seen to," he growled.

Mike said, "Go and get yourself a drink. There's time." He knew that she could not touch their whisky. Tamara put her coat on slowly, wincing.

"I shan't be long," she said and gave Mike a Judas kiss.

Her instructions were to get well away, out of the district, but she wanted to be on the spot. She ordered brandy, and needed it, but was too tense to feel its benefit. If she had twisted that dial too far, the police would already be in the house when the bomb went off. And they would be as unprepared as Mike and Rory.

The yearning maiden's eyes were soulfully, perpetually turned towards the row of bottles upside-down above their polished measures. Above them, the hands of the clock jerked. Ten seconds, nine, eight, seven—and the end of the maiden's long contemplation.

When the dust settled, Tamara joined the publican and his other customer at the door. They all knew better than to go nearer the ruins.

"There may be more to come," the publican said.

The street lights were all smashed. Nothing was left of the houses but rubble and dust. Tamara had not been sure how strong the bomb's explosive charge would be nor how fragile its surroundings. Mike and Rory's planned target had been smaller, but probably tougher.

The sirens of official vehicles approached, and a crowd was assembling, but nobody was keen to come very close.

"All condemned anyway," a woman said, and another remarked that nobody had been living there for weeks.

"I'd better be getting home," Tamara said. The publican patted her on the back and advised hot-water bottles and sweet tea.

"Clinical shock," he told her knowingly. "I saw a lot of it during the war."

Tamara slipped through the crowd and along to the main road, where nobody was taking much notice of the noise or of the fire-engines and police cars speeding by. Londoners were getting used to big bangs again.

Mike and Rory must have been killed instantly. Tamara wondered, as so often before, whether it had been as quick for Ian. She felt no sympathy, neither for Mike with whom she had lived and slept, nor for Rory, who had disliked but trusted her. She felt no guilt. She was unsullied by the necessities of revenge; on the contrary, she felt cleansed by violence. If she had possessed a sword, she would have marked two notches on its blade.

Tamara took a taxi home to the other side of town. She lived on the attic floor of a house in South Kensington. After her long absence, piles of letters were waiting on the mat, but her family and friends had been told that she was away on an excavation.

She switched on the water-heater, looking forward to her first bath in weeks, and took a fish pie from the freezer. Mike and Rory had insisted on meat for every meal. She had left a wood fire laid in the grate before leaving home weeks before, and she put a match to it before going across to draw the curtains. She stood for a moment looking out at the clean and peaceful street, all bright stucco, wrought-iron balconies, and trailing plants. One of her neighbours was walking his dog around the block before bed, and some cats were quarrelling in the communal gardens. Outside the front door of the Cabinet Minister in the next house, the police constable reassuringly stood.

Ian had died to preserve all this. But now his killers' colleagues had joined him.

The next morning Tamara went to work. Her office was in Savile Row, in a building that housed several Civil Service departments, including the Royal Commission for Ancient and Historical Monuments, for which Tamara worked. The drivers who overtook her bicycle whistled at the snub-nosed, yellow-haired girl with the brief-case in her carrier, and when she passed them again in traffic jams she waved back. The streets sparkled after the previous night's rain. Solid houses exuded security, thick-leaved parks invited relaxation. This did not look like a place where bombers planned terror. Nor did Tamara Hoyland look like what she was: an archaeologist, a civil servant—and a spy.

TAMARA'S SUCCESS in her first mission in the field was for private recognition only. In Mr. Black's eyes she had not exactly failed, herself unsuspected and her quarry dead, but things had not worked out according to his plan of arrest and trial. But he admitted forgivingly that the state would be spared considerable expense.

"I sometimes ask myself whether we only bring malefactors to justice to provide a Roman holiday for the newspaper reading public." He sighed and seemed about to embark on his next theme when his telephone buzzed. Tamara waited with some impatience. On her own desk, two floors down, several corridors along, piles of work awaited her delayed attention.

Tamara could still remember her initial surprise at Mr. Black's room; it had temporarily distracted her from absorbed grief. For she had read enough thrillers to know what the office of a Secret Service's middle manager should be like. He should be a distinguished-looking man, perhaps a retired rear-admiral. His work place should be disguised as the branch office of a faintly seedy business, and grey-faced men should come in through the kitchens of a restaurant next door to discuss their dirty tricks.

Tamara had expected only condolences when she had received a note inviting her to call on Mr. M. Black, Works

Department. She was a conventional civil servant at the time, qualified as an archaeologist, and employed to study and record field monuments. She had known something of Ian's secret work, for he had not been as discreet with her as he should have been, but until he died she had been more amused than convinced by the idea of Mr. Black and the Works Department. In other circumstances the sight of Mr. Black's room would also have amused her, so redolent as it was of Civil Service anonymity; it could have been duplicated many times in Whitehall, on the South Bank, in any of those office blocks on prime sites in which government departments proliferate. Chipped grey filing cabinets, a square of dingy carpet, and a coat-rack announced the ostensible grade of the room's occupant, and it was not a high one. Yet Mr. Black's air of authority was undiminished by the camouflage of his surroundings.

Even with half her mind still at a graveside, Tamara's attention was easily caught by what Mr. Black had to say. She had not guessed it. Perhaps that was foolish. She was unprepared for the surge of primitive fury that swamped her on hearing that Ian's death had not been plain bad luck. She knew that he had been an agent. But he had led her to believe that his activities had been intellectual, not physical.

"He died for his country," Mr. Black affirmed. "When you have grown used to the idea, you will be comforted to know that he did not die from fate's caprice. That bullet had Ian Barnes's name on it."

"But how? How could it have had?"

"He was betrayed," Mr. Black said.

"By whom?"

"We don't know. The man with him, another of my people, was injured in the same explosion."

"Seriously?"

"Enough to incapacitate him for this work, though not for ordinary life. He's left the service."

"Doesn't he know who gave them away?"

"Does it matter? A criminal, a traitor, or a patriot? Whatever they call themselves, they are our enemies."

It was not patriotism that made Tamara willing to be recruited to the service in Ian's place.

"Revenge is a quite satisfactory motive," Mr. Black said primly. "To begin with at least."

Tamara was surprised that agents should be recruited from within the Civil Service. No more than Mr. Black and his office did it fit the preconceptions she had derived from fiction.

"Where better to recruit, after all?" Mr. Black asked. "In the old days the most ingenious spies came from the universities. But one would not stake much on the loyalty of some of the younger dons now. On the other hand, we still need the brains."

"But civil servants . . ." Tamara was in the habit of describing herself as an archaeologist. The title of civil servant seemed to carry with it connotations of interference, incompetence, idleness, and caution.

"You must be half my age, Miss Hoyland; yet you still believe the myths of my youth."

"Income tax inspectors? Men from the ministry?"

"May have as adventurous imaginations as anyone."

He was offering her a job; and a chance, perhaps, to avenge Ian Barnes. Or if not that, then a chance to risk a life that since his death seemed worthless.

"I should need to know a good deal more about it," she said cautiously. Mr. Black told her a good deal more about it, and most of what he offered was no more interesting than any other job. But it would be thought-consuming and would fill in the time no longer earmarked for domestic felicity. It seemed that her employers were obliged to release her for some of her working hours too, if she needed to spend more time on this "good work" than her official leisure periods allowed, just as they would if she were a local councillor or a magistrate. She would benefit, as Mr. Black did, from the anonymity of government employment, her work place open to visitors, her secretary paid on the clerical grades, her extra emoluments tactfully concealed from the finance officer. Mr. Black commuted to work as though he were indeed a principal in the Works Department, and he lived in the confident expectation of receiving the civil servant's OBE—"Bearing in mind," he said, "that the expression 'other buggers' efforts' will be particularly appropriate."

"Are there people doing this work all over the building?" Tamara asked.

"They are scattered throughout the Civil Service."

"Do they recognize each other? Is there a kind of secret handshake?"

"I, and my secretary Mrs. Uglow, and your own boss, who has signed the Official Secrets Act, will be the only repositories of your secret. Even my masters seldom know the identity of those whose information they use or whose gallantries they honour."

"With medals?"

"In cash. Ian Barnes's family will have been told that he took out insurance on special Civil Service terms."

"You'll do the same for me if I'm shot, will you?"

"You should not overdramatize. Very few of my young people encounter any danger. Their work is less exciting than it seems in fiction. In your case, it is the archaeologist's expertise in sifting and evaluating evidence that will be especially useful."

Tamara was to receive training of a physical kind all the same. Mr. Black had an open file before him, and

Tamara was disconcerted to realize that he knew all about her. Who would have asked sly questions of whom? Casual enquirers must have gone to her school in Devon, to the sports centre where she had learned gym and judo, to the tennis club on Damden Hill, to the Commonwealth Swimming Pool in Edinburgh where Tamara had swum as an undergraduate, to the Cambridge University Boat Club where she had rowed when she was a post-graduate student there. Tamara experienced the superstitious fear that a tribesman might feel on hearing his secret name, the name in which his soul resided, the knowledge of which gave power to his enemy.

In the following weeks and months Tamara's friends thought that she was attending a civil servants' health club, sweating out her sad preoccupations. But in a basement below the gym, swimming pool, and solarium, she was prepared for what the instructor called "a spot of turbulence."

Tamara was good at shooting, having begun on rabbits in her childhood, but was useless at aiming a throw. "No grenades for you, miss," the instructor said, marking her card with the lowest grade. She learned to defend herself with weapons and without, to construct a variety of sinister devices, and to disarm those made by others; she learned how to use innocent substances in ways their manufacturers did not intend and to be suspicious of signs that others might have done so; she learned how to attack as well as defend; and she developed a memory already trained in the precise recollection of archaeological detail. At the end of a winter she was qualified to set herself up as an assassin or a private eye, and when she went home to her parents in Devonshire for a wet March week-end, they congratulated themselves—too tactful to congratulate her—on what seemed a remarkable recovery. Tamara's father was a solicitor who had little time for psychological mishmash and took her improvement in looks and health with matter-of-fact approval. Her mother wondered how she was sublimating her grief. Mr. Hoyland stroked her shining hair, and Mrs. Hoyland admired its style. But Alexandra Hoyland kept to herself the thought that Tamara wore the familiar expression of a younger sister planning mischief.

Mischief? Or a public service?

Her first mission completed, Tamara could argue a case for its being neither or both. She wondered whether Mr. Black had realized how whole-heartedly she would throw herself into the Mike-and-Rory assignment. Had he perhaps saved them up for her, knowing that her wits would be sharpened by personal motivation? Or was it merely a chance that was lucky for her?

And now it seemed her qualifications were lucky. She was to start out again at once. Her protests about in-trays were waved aside. Her director accepted that she must go to Forway. She was, ostensibly, to start the survey of its antiquities—a useful archaeological task that was at the same time the best possible cover story.

"Cover story? For Forway?"

"Didn't you mention that you had been there with Ian Barnes?"

Tamara knew that she had not mentioned it; and knew equally well that Mr. Black knew all about it. Was there anything about her or Ian that he did not have in his file?

Ian had taken her home to Forway just once. It was the only time that their leaves coincided in the three years they had spent together. She had found the island frightening and claustrophobic. But Ian loved it. He went back whenever he could.

"I don't want to go there again," Tamara said. "I won't."

Mr. Black said, "You have the excuse of your survey work; and Ian's family and friends will talk to you. You are just right for the job."

"On Forway, for heaven's sake? What job?"

Mr. Black passed Tamara a sheet of photocopied paper. The quality of print was poor, but the words were legible. It was the announcement of Forway's Unilateral Declaration of Independence.

"This is a joke, isn't it?" Tamara said. "I mean, you can't be taking this seriously. I don't believe it. Forway's the remotest inhabited island in Europe. It's only got a handful of people living there. This is a practical joke."

Mr. Black admitted that he was inclined to agree, but it was the kind of joke that could turn sick or sour. "You go and see what's going on. It'll be like a holiday for you. After your hard time in the slums with those bombers."

"I can't go and spy on Ian's mother."

"You can. You will. Honour is dead. British officers shoot their enemies in the back. This is the twentieth century. You go and gather some information. Let's call it a watching brief."

TAMARA MANAGED TO CATCH the afternoon train. It was very full, and she had little space to arrange the papers she needed to study before arriving on Forway in the guise of a specialist in its antiquities. The conversations around her seemed more interesting. It was always amusing that people travelled together as though they were in some kind of limbo where nobody would recognize the names or be interested in the details they described.

Two free-lance journalists were sharing Tamara's table. They were on their way to Forway too, though nothing that they said implied that they had heard whispers of political upheavals there. Mr. Black had not told Tamara how he came by the copy of the notice he had shown her, but he had said that nobody outside the island knew of it, and that she was not to let on that she knew of it inside the island. These journalists were very grumpy about the miseries of second-class travel and the tribulations of the free-lance. They tittered desperately about the coming ferry crossing, gesturing out of the window where even the dead elm trees tossed in a strengthening wind.

"God knows where we'll stay when we get to the bloody place," the young man said.

"You don't suppose they demand proof of a bed before

they let you land?" exclaimed his companion. "That happened to me on a Greek island once."

"Sleeping under a hedge, oh God."

"There will be by-laws." The woman was clanking with necklaces and loaded down by cameras. Her pointed nails were scarlet. Would she look smart or silly on Forway, Tamara wondered, twitching at her own jeans.

She recognized the man suddenly. Carl Hawker: the man who had come to fame by revealing the identities of Communist spies, past and present, and hinting at those of the future. How cross he would have been to hear that it had taken her from London to Exeter to attach a name to those features.

"Mary and I had a holiday there two years ago," he said despondently. "That's why they thought I should cover it now. It rains for one thousand four hundred and forty minutes every day."

"Jolly for campers."

"The campers who are fools enough to go there deserve what they get, which is a pitch on a soaking sponge. We put up with a peasant woman in a shack. The guide-book said it was a voyage out of the twentieth century."

The train's terminus was at Penzance, where the passengers for Forway were decanted onto a platform near the pier. The ferry boat looked a frail cockle-shell for the eight-hour crossing, and it was already bouncing up and down in a minatory fashion. The two journalists evidently relied on alcohol, and Carl Hawker was heard loudly recommending a mixture of port and brandy. Tamara swallowed a double dose of Stugeron. Her distaste for and distrust of the sea had been one of the major points of difference between her and Ian. And this boat was peculiarly unattractive. It sailed once a week, a shallow-bottomed tub—there was no deep-water anchorage at Forway—rusty and paint-chipped, reeking of diesel and vomit. At one time the British government had subsidized the ferry service. When the subsidy dwindled, the cost of goods sent to and from Forway became not simply ridiculous but impossible. A year ago the subsidy had been withdrawn, and the ferry company said that its loss-making service would soon cease as a consequence. No alternative suggestions about supplying the island had been made, although it was dependent upon its imports of such staples as paraffin and diesel fuel, sugar, salt, tea, coffee, alcoholic drinks, and everything made of metal, quite apart from the fruit and vegetables that could not grow in its peaty wastes. To be completely reliant on home-produced goods, few as they were, such as salted fish, feathers, and fulmar oil, knitwear and harsh cloth, tough meat and sour cheese, as the islanders had briefly been during the two world wars, would have been intolerable to a generation educated to the expectation of comforts by television. A leader in the *Times* had used the dread words "Evacuation of the island's population." Shortly after that announcement, Ian had taken Tamara to Forway. Moored within the small harbour was a craft belonging to an international mineral-exploration company. Its elegant paintwork and gleaming brass showed up the squalor of the ferry. It looked as though there might be resources on Forway after all—for some.

No sleeping berths were available on the ferry. Tamara found herself a corner on a torn leatherette bench and wrapped herself in her duffle coat. The lounge, as it was grandly called, was decorated with posters inviting visitors to sample the simple pleasures of Forway: rock climbing, walking, nature study. A picture, surely in breach of the Trades Descriptions Act, showed bikini-clad girls running across a golden beach. In fact, unlike the Isles of Scilly, Forway was not edged with flour-soft sand. It had two stony coves, delightful for geologists but neither safe for bathers nor comfortable for baskers, and one small shell beach on which for all but about seven days of the year the wind rasped abrasives against any uncovered skin.

It was too noisy and dim to read. Tamara sunk her chin down into the rough warmth of her coat. Last time she made this crossing, she had pillowed her face on Ian's shoulder. He had been too excited about going home to sleep.

What was it about that bleak rock that enchanted its natives? Tamara had tried to understand—indeed, had tried to love it too; for in a lifetime with Ian she could expect to spend months if not years on Forway. She had gone there expecting it to be like the Scillies, which she knew well from childhood holidays and which were obviously lovable. In Scilly, jewel-coloured islands surround a limpid lagoon; subtropical plants flower in scented gardens. But not even a myth maker could ever have thought that Forway was a promised land, Ultima Thule though it might be. The climate was hostile, the soil sour, and the island had never been a welcome landfall. It is an isolated rock with a cluster of smaller, barren rocks around it. Their base slopes into the depths. Like St. Paul's Rocks in the South Atlantic Ocean, it is one of the few exceptions to an almost universal rule, that oceanic islands have a volcanic origin. In the remote past, unimaginable stresses in the midst of the earth must have pushed this rocky mass upwards until the island protruded from the deep sea. It has been described, in terms ranging from the cool to the appalled, by numerous travellers. Any ship forced into its minimal shelter would leave as soon as possible. Any mariner who survived shipwreck on this inhospitable shore—and the shores were exceeded in danger only by the savage inhabitants for most of recorded history —stayed until they were rescued by chance transport. For-

way might have been a desert island for all the means of escape it offered.

Forway's history was vague, but for the certainty that
it was brutish and nasty. When the British navy smoked out
the nest of pirates there in the eighteenth century, the
wretched peasants who had been those pirates' slaves found
their shacks destroyed also. For a while it was used as a
prison, the Northern Hemisphere's answer to St. Helena, but
no competent governor would stay there, and without
proper control the prisoners themselves became wreckers
and pirates. A garrison was stationed there during the
Napoleonic wars but was soon withdrawn when its men mu-
tinied and escaped; they said that it would even be better to
be pressed into the navy. During the world wars of the present century, garrisons were maintained. Small detachments
of soldiers grumbled their way through four boring years.
They were given the rations of men on overseas service.

The suppression of piracy by the British navy had managed to reduce the inhabitants of Forway to wretched pov-
erty although wrecks continued to bring some harvest to the
island. But, for food, the population became dependent on
the potato crop. When that failed in Ireland, it failed in
Forway too. But somehow the islanders survived, self-
sufficient and self-supporting—just—and self-limiting. The
small nucleus of population was reinvigorated by a man
with a mission from Glasgow. Septimus Lisle arrived in
1887 with his prayer-book, Bible, and a tramp steamer full
of equipment. Ten years later his burgeoning civilization
was augmented by some shipwrecked mariners who chose
to stay where they had been succoured. A few years pre-
viously they would have been more likely to meet death
than rescue on those shores. By the turn of the century the
huddle of shacks had turned into a miniscule town, with
one or two slate roofs showing among those that were

turfed and with a chapel that was well attended on Sundays and used as a schoolroom on weekdays. One of the Lisle sons had brought back a brass plate from London where he had gone to train as a lawyer. A doctor had left the Cunard line and settled on Forway. A nurse was sent by a Bible missionary society.

To a British government of the late twentieth century, Forway was merely one of the many inhabited islands off the coast of the United Kingdom, its legal position anomalous but—until recently—unchallenged, its desirability, with no natural resources, without enough flat land for a runway or enough deep water for a harbour, dubious. If it had been uninhabited it could have been used, no doubt, for strategic purposes; or to experiment with germ warfare.

Gaunt, bleak, inhospitable, and lonely. It was easy to understand, Tamara thought, how that judgement, quoted in Parliament and in the national press, could be made of Forway. She had made it herself. No wonder it was regarded as a punishment station by the customs officer doing a three-year stretch or by the policeman on his two-year tour of duty. Even the surveyor, camping on The Hill last year, with his taciturn team, for undisclosed purposes, had loosened up enough one night in The Hotel to admit that the best thing that could happen to the dump would be—but at that point he came to himself and would not say which disagreeable fate he would recommend for Forway.

But to the island nurse, Jeannie Foggo, who had so badly missed the island every day of her training; to Dr. Thetis Lisle, who had not quite realized how much she longed for it until she got back from her seven-year stint in London; to the Yetts men, farming the tiny steep fields first taken in by their grandfather; to the Aragons, that extended clan descending from an ancestor who had survived the shipwreck of his galleon in Armada year and stayed where the sea had washed him; to Kirstie Windows, now asleep on the floor of the lounge of the SS *Islander* by Tamara Hoyland's feet: to them all, Forway was warm in welcome, and homely. But in the dawn, when Tamara saw through the damp mist the first glimpse of those striated, dun-coloured rocks rising like a wall of death from the Atlantic, she felt a chill that was not entirely caused by remembering what Mr. Black expected of her.

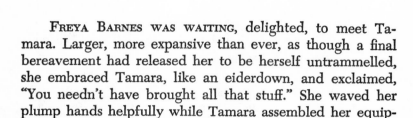

FREYA BARNES WAS WAITING, delighted, to meet Tamara. Larger, more expansive than ever, as though a final bereavement had released her to be herself untrammelled, she embraced Tamara, like an eiderdown, and exclaimed, "You needn't have brought all that stuff." She waved her plump hands helpfully while Tamara assembled her equipment. "All Ian's tools are still here. Have you come to dig?"

"Just a field survey for the time being."

"If you find a treasure, we won't let you take it away to London this time."

Five years before, a remote government that never guessed the worm might turn had refused to let the Forway men retain a silver hoard from the early Christian period which had turned up under a plough. Its removal and display by the British Museum was regarded as an unforgiven robbery.

Freya linked her cushiony arm in Tamara's. "My frog is having its oil changed. We'll collect some food." Freya's old Bedford van, her "Frog," more like a motorized wheelbarrow than a car, was in the open-sided shed that served as the Forway garage, and beside it one of the Yetts men nodded to Tamara as she deposited her baggage. He was talking to a man with a beard who was pointing out faults in a battered ex-post-office van. Freya waved but walked on. She

said to Tamara, "You'll meet him soon enough. Rik Gerson.
They weren't here last time you came. Lena Gerson is a sort
of cousin of mine, and they have bought the Peter Aragons'
place. The Peter Aragons have gone to live in Majorca."

"Are the Gersons farming?"

"They try to be self-sufficient, but one does meet them
buying tinned spaghetti. The fox takes the chickens, the
cow is dry. Lena tries very hard to be part of Forway. But
as an outsider . . ."

"But if she's a relation of yours?"

"Pedro and I were not natives, as you know. We were
not accepted overnight. But Pedro was so lovable. Of course
everyone here loved him. Lena Gerson . . . I haven't any
other relatives left. So perhaps . . ." The old woman broke
off and stared at the sea, refusing to squeeze any tears from
her eyes. They were the same brilliant turquoise as Ian's.

"How do the Gersons manage to live here?" Tamara
enquired.

"Oh, they have a little of their own."

It was easy to imagine how hard the Forway men
would have tried to discover that little's source, the
postmistress holding letters up to the light to try reading the signature on cheques, the neighbours dropping hints
and asking questions, those scrapes at each individual's reti-
cence that make up life in enclosed communities.

"Lena spins and knits wool, too," Freya added.

"While he knits their spinach, I suppose?"

"That kind of thing. And they have fixed up some of
the outbuildings as holiday lets, but I don't think that is giving much satisfaction. And then they have a little printing-
press."

"They can't make that farm worse than it was," Tamara
said. She had heard on her first visit about that branch of
the Aragon family, feckless and uncooperative, with a high

proportion of defective children. There had been some tale of a son tethered to a kennel and fed on scraps. Though that was half a century ago, memories were long on Forway.

Tamara carried Freya's purchases on a slow progress between the three shops. Everybody had apparently been reminded of Tamara in advance, for she was greeted by name and welcomed with the implication that she belonged here, because Ian Barnes had belonged. She smiled back at faces to which she could only put surnames, and only that because there were few to choose from. Families on Forway were called Yetts, Aragon, Lisle, Windows, and Foggo. The Barnes family was a late addition, and nobody else would bear that name now. And there was the settler Selwyn Paull, who had a son in London. But there had been so much intermarriage between the clans that they were little differentiated in social life. Still, Ian had told her, there was a tall dark strain of Yetts men, a red-faced, blond, stocky Windows type; Tamara doubted now, as she had the previous year, whether she would ever be able to think of most of these islanders as individuals. Forway had stamped them all. They used the same Christian names as each other too. Fred, John, Humphrey, Godfrey, and Magnus, for boys; Thetis (after the first girl whose parents liked the name of a shipwrecked steamer), Jean, Kirstie, and Anona.

A woman Tamara was sure she had not seen before was buying meat in front of Freya. Her appearance could only be the result of long avoidance of mirrors. Her cheekbone was badly bruised, and when her sleeve fell back her arm showed black and blue. She smelt acrid, as though her clothes were impregnated with old food, and though her macintosh and skirt had evidently once been expensive there were great rips in them now.

One of Europe's last witch-hunts had taken place on

Forway. This woman looked like the reincarnation of the wretched creature, who had died at last when she fled into the sea and was prevented by thrown stones from struggling back to land. But now the voice was purest Knightsbridge.

"Four pounds of the sirloin, Mrs. Windows, please," she ordered. "Well hung if you please. The last joint was not quite to my liking."

"Very good, Mrs. Anholt."

"And please be so good as to send up some marrow bones for the dogs too." They watched her as she went serenely across to the shop where Fred Yetts was selling newspapers, paraffin, wellington boots, and all the stock of an old-fashioned general store.

"Real lady-of-the-manor stuff," Mrs. Windows said thoughtfully. "Godfrey Lisle always pays her accounts, you know, Mrs. Barnes. He's her lawyer, of course. I can just remember her old grandfather—and her, too, in the old days. But it shouldn't be allowed, all the same."

"Nonie Anholt grew up on Forway, in The Castle," Freya told Tamara. "She came back here to live a little while ago."

"It isn't right, that's what I say," Mrs. Windows said. "Did you see the bruises today, Mrs. Barnes? The man she has up at The Castle does that. Beats her up. I've spoken to Mr. Lisle about it. And I've done more too. I've written to her son. In Camberley. I got the address from a postcard she sent. I told him to come and take care of his poor old mother. You wouldn't believe what it's like up at The Castle, Mrs. Barnes, you wouldn't really. I had to deliver myself last week, John was away in Cork having his teeth seen to, and the mess up there! Ridden with vermin. It shouldn't be allowed."

"Who is to stop her?" Freya Barnes asked. "She prefers it to somewhere sanitized on the mainland."

"Have you seen her cousin? That man staying at The Castle? Irish—I heard his voice. You can see he doesn't treat her right, can't you? How she looks . . . !"

"I remember Nonie Anholt years ago," Freya said. "Before the war, even. You've never seen such a pretty, polished creature. So frivolous and superficial. Never thought about anything but men and clothes. Once at a party in Oxford, she had a hat with a feather curling all down the side of her face. I can see her now, blowing it out of her mouth . . . even Pedro thought she was charming, and he didn't often like stupid women. I'd forgotten she had a son. Did you say you'd written to him?"

"I did that," Mrs. Windows replied virtuously. "I told him straight. It's your duty, I said, your duty to come and see after your old mother. That Irishman . . ."

Outside the shop, pursued by self-righteous chatter, Freya and Tamara watched Nonie Anholt staggering ahead of them.

"Tamara, promise you won't ever do anything for my good," Freya said suddenly. "If I become like poor Nonie there, for instance—you must always remember it's my own life."

"People like that Mrs. Windows are very powerful, aren't they?" Tamara said. "Buoyed up by the certainty of their own rectitude."

"That's always been the trouble with Forway, or so people say. The women govern. Their much-discussed opinions are voiced by their men as new-minted decisions."

"A gynocracy."

"Which is becoming a gerontocracy. We are all too old. *Isola Geriatrica* . . ."

The van was ready, and Freya drove with fine insouciance along the track and hillside to her home. She left the van apparently at random out on the hill.

Behind a wind-break of woven fencing and Californian pines, a garden thrived in the temperate climate. Ian used to say that he was colder in a London spring than ever in a Forway winter. But the wind was incessant. Freya's plants, and indeed all growth on the island, were sculpted by it. Wind speeds faster than a hundred miles an hour had several times broken instruments set to measure them, and sometimes solid clouds of spray would blow from one side of the island to the other.

On the bench outside the cottage a black cat was asleep. One side of the double door—designed to push open whatever the wind direction—was propped wide. The laboratory, across the yard, already looked abandoned, a depressing reminder, but Freya did not glance at it.

In Pedro Barnes's lifetime the house was scattered with the belongings he left in his wake: pipes, matches, books, papers, tools, specimens, coffee cups, irresistible driftwood, and the materials for half-completed experiments. These days the kitchen was tidy and smelt of lavender instead of cooking.

"Lovely smell," Tamara said.

"I can't smell anything these days. Old age."

"Chain-smoking more likely."

"Too late to stop now," Freya said.

The low-ceilinged living-room would have been a good setting for a more fey, more folk-tale-type figure than Freya. Ian's mother had become so fat as to seem dropsical. Her ankles swelled out above her shoes, her tiny hands dangled from trunklike arms. A famous portrait of her as the young wife of a famous professor, by Kokoschka, hung in the Courtauld Gallery, but she looked like a distortion of it now. Generations of Pedro Barnes's students had written verses to the beautiful woman whose shadow lurked in the grotesque flesh. Many of them were at retiring age themselves by now, and she was beginning to feature in memoirs, a popular and influential hostess at university festivities.

Pedro Barnes was within seven years of retirement when Freya found that she was expecting a child. Their giggling friends had suppressed their mirth for long enough to say that it was no joke at her age. Her contemporaries, now grandparents, were sympathetic at the prospect of being landed with a baby that could not be handed back to its young parents when it became tiresome.

But Pedro and Freya welcomed Ian as the old woman welcomed Tom Thumb. Pedro retired early, they enlarged their holiday home on Forway, and brought their son up on the island. And now Freya was the only one left.

"I should have come to see you even if they hadn't sent me to do a field survey," Tamara said guiltily. She had not considered Freya's loneliness before.

Freya always knew what to say. Just now—nothing. She sat in the cane chair with its coracle back, which Pedro had ordered for her from the Hebrides. She rested her bulbous ankles on a faded tapestry stool and showered cigarette ash about her. As always she wore a vast canvas smock that covered layers of clothes and rolls of fat. She had whitened tennis shoes on her oddly small feet, and pressing into the skin of her fourth finger was Pedro's gold and onyx signet ring.

Tamara thought with determination about her work; she would keep her mind upon impersonal subjects. The field survey: that would be a pleasure—after all, she was really an archaeologist. And the job for which the field survey was a cover? That seemed even more ridiculous now that she was here on Forway. There were no signs of unrest or agitation that she could see. No posters, no huddled groups of conspiratorial whisperers, no sidelong glances, no conversations abruptly broken off—none of the evidence of conspiracy that had been described to her. Perhaps Mr. Black thought that she needed a holiday.

Lena Gerson came into the cottage without knocking and assumed a welcoming air towards Tamara, as though she were the hostess both on Forway and in this house. She did not look like the conventional escaper from urban corruption. Tamara had expected her to be in the uniform of those who reject the works of civilization, clothes partly homespun and partly made on rather expensive machines but all decorated with patterns derived from either nature or the Third World. Lena Gerson looked like a highly competent secretary—and turned out to have been one. She spoke of her job in London with enough traces of wistfulness in her voice for Tamara to ask, "Do you miss it?"

Lena smiled at Freya and said quickly, "No, no, not a bit. We're terrifically happy here. We were both longing to get away."

Lena went through to the kitchen, and Tamara watched through the open door as she bent to take a nylon overall out of her bag and put it and some rubber gloves on before beginning to clean the sink and wipe over the cooker.

"How nice for you that Lena has come to live here," Tamara said.

"Yes, she is very kind to me," Freya agreed.

"I have brought you a turnip pie, Freya," Lena called. "There's plenty for two of you."

"You make too much for me, dear. I shared the last one with Sergeant Hicks." Freya lowered her voice and whispered to Tamara, "I can't eat that vegetarian food. It gives me indigestion. But it's kindly meant."

"And shall I throw away this bit of cheese? It looks a bit past it to me?" Lena Gerson's voice was high, with slightly flattened vowels. It was the voice of a suburban housewife on a phone-in programme asking the experts how to remove stains from her table-cloths. It sounded strangely foreign here.

Tamara felt restless; had James Bond been inhibited by social embarrassment from doing what he wanted? Would he have sat politely giving a hostess the requisite amount of attention before going off to his own work? I should have brought some knitting, she thought. What have Ian's mother and I in common to converse about now?

"You have come here at an exciting time, Tamara," Freya Barnes said after a while. Tamara opened her eyes wide, in assumed incomprehension. Lena Gerson came in, smoothing cream into her hands.

"Do tell her about it, Freya," she urged. "She's sure to be safe."

"Oh, Tamara is one of the family," Freya said.

"But what is this?" Tamara said. "What's the great secret?"

"You know that they have found oil deposits in this part of the western approaches."

"But that has been announced, surely, it's no secret."

"What has been kept secret is the plans for extracting it. It's only because Selwyn Paull still has his contacts in Whitehall that we know."

"Isn't it done with oil rigs? I've seen pictures—"

"Their plan for this area is rather different."

"You won't believe it, Tamara," Lena Gerson said eagerly.

"They want to evacuate all the islanders," Freya went on, "all the natives forced off the island, and the whole of Forway used as a rock-based oil rig. Have all their camps and everything here, devote the whole place to it."

"Isn't it incredible?" Lena said. "Can you imagine it? Just think—at Sullem Vog, on Shetland, their pay-roll is five thousand people! They've built two whole villages for them, quite apart from housing some in a converted car ferry. That's what an oil terminal takes. And that's what they want to do here."

"Are you sure?" Tamara asked.

"They have just a few more days to change their plans. Until Friday," Freya said sternly.

"What happens then?"

"The Visit. The first Royal Visit to Forway ever."

"I still think it's a shame we can't have one of the important ones. The queen, say, or . . ." Lena grumbled.

"It will be the last Royal Visit too," Freya went on firmly. "Unless the Visitor brings a message that the oil plan has been dropped."

"What then—if there's no such message?"

"We make our Unilateral Declaration of Independence. Our independence from all three of the governments that have staked a claim to Forway. France, Ireland, and the United Kingdom."

Lena Gerson's hands were clasped under her chin. She said, "It is all so exciting."

"I shall invest Pedro's money in a Trust for Forway."

In the days when she and Ian Barnes had talked about marriage, the Barnes wealth had been one of Tamara's causes for hesitation. Pedro Barnes had become staggeringly rich during his retirement. He had patented several inventions of practical application in industry. The most lucrative, ironically, was indispensable for the extraction of oil. Pedro and Freya Barnes, and now Freya on her own, could have gone to live anywhere in the world; yet they chose this chunk of weather-battered rock. Tamara had no moral scruples about wealth, but she wanted to live a life that was normal by the standards of her class. "I am a product of the puritan ethic," she used to say ruefully to Ian. He had been similarly conditioned. They wanted to live in a house of no more than comfortable size, they wanted only occasional domestic help, they wanted to send their children to local schools, without the constant fear of burglars or kidnappers. They both wanted to need their jobs. "I wasn't cut out to be rich," Tamara had said. Ian used to reply, "We can always give it away," but they had both known it would be hard. "I wish I had your problems," Tamara's sister, Alexandra, who was married to a teacher and had three small children, had commented. "You can always give it to me."

Now it seemed that Freya was indeed about to give the wealth away.

"It sounds a bit drastic," Tamara said mildly.

"We can see no alternative."

"But won't anyone else—"

"We have had them all. The conservationists, archaeologists, ornithologists, biologists, botanists—Forway has been a living laboratory for years. But only money gives power."

"You have to live here," Lena Gerson said, "to understand how wonderful it is. There is something about the way of life . . ." She took a compact from her bag and examined her face carefully before painting on a renewal of lipstick. "I must go back. Rik's waiting." She gathered herself together in a feminine flurry and left, waving as she walked past the window.

"Your cousin doesn't look quite naturalized yet," Tamara remarked.

"I doubt whether she likes Forway as much as her husband does," Freya agreed. "I didn't myself when Pedro decided to come here permanently. Holidays were one thing, all the year round quite another. Still, look at me now."

"Rik Gerson is the away-from-it-all type, is he?"

"Seems to be. And I must say that Lena is taking a lot

of trouble over me—not all in the hope of a little legacy, I'm sure. In any case, she and Rik quite agree with our independence plans. They are as involved as anyone."

"I can see you are all quite committed."

"After all, darling," Freya said, "what would I do as a lonely multimillionairess all alone away from Forway? This is what Pedro would have wanted me to do. Ian, too. Ian. I used to warn him to drive carefully. Killed outright, they said. Ian . . ." Her plump face loosened, its lines slackening as though an internal strength had been relaxed. She mumbled indistinguishable words and twisted her hands together. In a few moments she said, her voice weaker, "I get confused sometimes." She lit another cigarette, not commenting on the almost unsmoked one that Tamara had stubbed out, when it fell from her fingers.

Tamara said gently, "What will the islanders do with the money?"

"We are making elaborate arrangements. You'd be surprised. Boarding schools in Switzerland, a helicopter of our own, a proper cottage hospital. In future we shall ask nothing from the big powers. It's little enough they gave when we needed it, withdrawing our ferry from England, refusing us a scheduled flight. We shall leave them to fight over territorial waters without us. It will be a new world."

"I'm afraid you will find snags," Tamara said soberly.

"I dare say. One always does. But world opinion will be on our side. We have arranged press coverage too. It will make a good story—David and Goliath. Come along, darling, I'll show you your room." Freya took the weight on her wrists, heaving herself up, and led Tamara to what had been Ian's bedroom. Tamara remembered it well. Could they have gone on being happy here? She was uneasy at the strangeness of the island. This could never have been my

home, she thought, but knew that Ian would have wished to
live in it.

Tamara put her clothes into the drawers now emptied
of Ian's property. She disposed her gadgets. The miniature
camera in a box of tampons, the various eavesdropping kits
rolled into her underwear. The lipstick and the deodorant
spray had false bottoms and dangerous contents. She could
not imagine needing any of them here. The simplest
weapon was sold in stationers' shops, a razor-blade set into a
plastic handle. That went into a canvas satchel along with
the spring measure, the clinometer, and the thirty-metre
tape. The ring on the end of that could be unscrewed to fit
on her finger, with a lethally sharp point jutting upwards.

She hesitated with her hand on a tin of powder but decided to go the whole hog while she was about it. She spilt
some talc in strategic places and used spit to stick a couple
of hairs across the drawers. She felt uneasily that all she
could be was conscientious, like a student whose work was
bad but gained points for effort.

I am Magnus Paull, the son of Sir Selwyn Paull. I was born on Forway and spent periods of my childhood there. My most recent trip to Forway had been about a year before Tamara was sent there. I was about due to pay a filial visit in any case and it was convenient to be out of London just then since the girl who had been living with me for the last few months was beginning to nag about marriage and mortgages, and we had consequently agreed to part. I reminded her of our initial agreement that there would be no ill feeling if things didn't work out. She thought things were working out. However, I could not at that time imagine the woman with whom I would be prepared to stay for ever. There never seemed to be a shortage of candidates for the left-hand side of my large bed and the row of fitted cupboards in my entrance hall. It seemed wise to leave the girl a few days to move herself and her belongings out. "You may be the bee's knees in bed, Magnus," she shouted after me, "but one of these days you'll find a girl who wants more than just your pretty face."

I flew as far as Cork from London Heathrow. The wait in Cork was supposed to be two hours and turned out to be much longer, which should not have surprised me; I had heard the weather forecast before leaving London. "And now here is a gale warning. Southerly gale eight, strengthening severe gale force nine, sea areas Rockall, Bailey . . . sea areas Shannon, Forway, Irish Sea, severe gale force nine strengthening storm force ten, veering easterly later."

I sat morosely in the bar, jostled by passengers waiting for an overdue flight to Aberdeen. Airports are the century's purgatory: misery on the way to better or worse. A girl with rainbow-coloured hair tried chatting me up, but she had bad teeth and legs. These mass-produced people were unspeakably depressing. As often, I reminded myself that if one did not live in the century of the common man, one would not live in the century of aspirin and piped water either. How I hate the human race, how I hate its silly face . . . especially when it chatters about the trivia a quick survey revealed: golf handicaps, had one remembered to turn the gas off, could one buy Marlboros in Scotland, what would whisky cost there, the likelihood of rain, the certainty of delay. On my left a fat man and a sequinned woman were carrying on the Great Bores of Today double-glazing conversation. On my right a local man with a taxi driver's badge in his lapel was talking to a small Englishman in dirty jeans.

The Irish voice said, "So you're none the worse? No more than a dunt on the head . . ."

"We haven't regretted it for a moment. Of course it costs a fortune . . ."

"There were after-effects. They say I have memory loss."

"The saving on your fuel bills, what with the price of oil these days . . ."

"How can they tell about your memory? What do you forget?"

"When you come to sell, it raises the value . . ."

"When I say that I've forgotten."

The Irishman whistled. "That's neat. A blighty one."

"The other real plus, it keeps the noise out . . ."

"What's a blighty one?"

"Course you have to be careful not to get taken for a ride. Plenty of cowboys . . ."

"In the First World War. A wound that got you sent home for the duration. They used to shoot their own feet off."

"Too many rip-off merchants around these days, conning the householder . . ."

"I didn't hit myself on the head."

"And of course it's a real deterrent in case of burglars."

"A really scientific job," the Irishman said, clapping the other man on the back.

The tannoy announced the departure of the helicopter for Forway. The fat householder went on indefatigably, "It needn't spoil the look of the place. After a day or so you hardly notice it."

I stood up and so did the small man in jeans. He went over to help a depressed-looking girl with expensive luggage and London clothes. The three of us were the only passengers, but it was too noisy to talk even if we had wanted to. The machine sprang up and down as though the sky was a trampoline. Later in the day my travelling companions were identified to me: Rik and Lena Gerson, coming househunting to Forway.

There is no such thing as a terminal or heliport on the island. The machine simply comes down on a flattish piece of ground—one of the few there are—marked out with a concrete H, and the passengers scurry to or from it, ducking under the whirlwind of the rotors; the helicopter makes a quick turn-around.

Freya and Pedro Barnes had been waiting in their old van, and I passed them as they went to the helicopter. Pedro carried Freya's luggage, and she limped badly, leaning on two sticks. Since I had last seen her, Ian Barnes had been killed in a car crash, so it was not surprising that she had aged.

Only Freya climbed in. By the time the helicopter was heading north again and one could hear oneself speak, Pedro was by my side, offering to drop me at my father's place. Petrol and diesel are in short supply on the island, and people seldom drive anywhere, but Freya had been very crippled. "They are giving her a tin hip," Pedro told me. "She's got so bad, she can hardly move."

"You not going to keep her company?"

"I am going over in a couple of weeks. It's when she's convalescing that Freya will need me, and I've got some work to finish."

Pedro did not look in the best of health himself. He had always been a small man, but with bright eyes and a clear, olive skin that originally led his friends to address Peter Seton Barnes by the Spanish nickname of Pedro. Now his deeply lined face looked weather-beaten and worn.

I had written to them when Ian died, of course, and now I mumbled something again.

"He was a great loss to us," Pedro said simply. "I am afraid that it will leave Freya very much alone. She is fifteen years my junior, as you know."

There was a hard-bottomed though not surfaced strip known as The Road, some of the way across the hillside, and then a vestigial track that led past my father's cottage on the Aragon farm, and on to the Barnes's place. The van was so shaken by the wind that one continuously feared being overturned.

"Is anyone looking after you while Freya's away, Pedro? Shall I come and see you?"

"I can manage very well, my boy, thank you. I'm busy with some work for the next few days. I shall be glad to see

you after that." A courteous way of telling me to leave him
alone. I slid back the van door into the wind's attack and
leaped out to close it as fast as I could. But a little thing like
wind would not keep my father indoors. He came out to
greet me, drawing in deep breaths as though the harsh air
did him good. Unlike Pedro Barnes, he was blooming. I allowed the thought to cross my mind that my own early
death would be unlikely to affect him as much as Ian's had
Pedro; my fault, or his? The Aragons' two dogs ran across
the farmyard, barking hysterically, and my father shoved
the collie away with a shining shoe.

"The Aragons are selling up," he bawled and did not
lower his voice very much in the shelter of the cottage to
tell me that some cousins of Freya Barnes were coming over
to look at the place. "They can't make much more of a mess
than Peter Aragon has, that's one thing," he said. "Sign of
the times though, the old families leaving and young townees coming here to live."

The wind strength increased in the night, and the next
day was a full-blown storm force eleven. Once it is force
twelve, they call it a hurricane. The weather seemed ap-
pallingly wild to me; but then, I had never been on the island during one of those storms that are used as measure-
ment of the passing time—"the year of the great storm," as
people would say. I had been told that after such days,
people are left literally deaf, sometimes for weeks, from the
cacophony of pounding sea, howling wind, and thunder.

I stayed indoors. I was past the age of having to obey
my father's injunctions to blow the cobwebs away. I had
plenty to read, since I was preparing to write a book about
Younghusband, and I tried to divert my father's disgusted
appeals by seeming abstracted in scholarly concentration.
The house, and all the things in it, shook and rattled. Few
structures on Forway rise above one storey and some are

dug into the ground so as to present only a smooth line of roof to the west. This gale was, unusually, from the south-east, and treacherously it found every corner or protrusion or gap.

Some of the time it rained, and then the water was driven against the windows with the blinding violence of one of these mechanical car washes. In the dry intervals I watched through the newly clean glass how everything that grew was forced horizontal and how the mountainous seas—visible from every point on the island—were crashing in avalanches over the coast.

Occasionally I caught sight of Peter Aragon or his wife, bent double against the onslaught, running across the farm-yard to the sheds. There could hardly be worse conditions for the prospective purchasers to view the property in. I saw them more than once, as they examined the structures of the farm. When I saw them coming huddled arm in arm from the hilltop, I thought scornfully that only townees born and bred would go for walks in this weather.

My father made several determined outings, but all were for some practical purpose. Once he went to call on Pedro Barnes, but he came back saying that the door was closed against callers. Once or twice I went with my father, though it offended him to hear me imply that I was better able to carry loads of peat than he. It was still midwinter-chilly on Forway. In London there had been tulips and lilac in the park and pink May-blossom outside my study win-dows.

On the fifth day the wind dropped to force seven. I paid duty calls and was told how like my mother, stroke fa-ther, I looked, and what unseasonable weather we were having. Neither the ferry nor the helicopter had called since the day I came, but Forway men are used to being cut off from supplies, sometimes for weeks at a time, and it was only luxuries that we went without. At least there was the radio link nowadays. A lot of people could remember when the only way to get messages off the island in bad weather had been to attract the attention of passing shipping (which was hard, since no sensible captain willingly passed anywhere near Forway) or had been, quite literally, to send messages in bottles. The St. Kildans had developed a system of sending message canoes, like kayaks, and the prevailing currents and wind did tend to wash them up on Scottish shores. Forway's bottles were too seldom found for any more sophisticated conveyances to have been invented. Of most there was never a trace. Occasionally children from far away places like the Baltic coast or the Canary Islands would write asking for rewards.

Forway runs with surface water in heavy rain, which drains the soil and seeds with it into the sea. I was keen to leave this barren, battered rock, and on the sixth day I told my father that I would be off when the helicopter next called.

On the seventh day the air was suddenly still. The sky was blue, the sea all brilliant peacock shades flecked with white. As always after such storms, the swell would take ages to settle but, to the eyes of one who did not intend to embark upon it, was very beautiful.

We had left Pedro undisturbed.

"He'll be busy inventing something profitable," my father said. "Amazing the way the feller makes his fortune by patenting some formula." I wondered whether the old man should be left alone through such a storm, but my father said huffily that Pedro was only two years older than he was. "I can cope, so can he," he insisted.

Dr. Thetis Lisle dropped in to check my father's blood pressure and said she had just come by the Barnes place. The outer door of Pedro's laboratory was still closed. He maintained the Oxford custom of sporting his oak. When that outside door was shut, it meant "Do not disturb."

"Yes, it was closed when I went up there the other day too," my father said.

"I expect he's working hard to get finished before he goes off to keep Freya company."

My father said, "Extraordinary brain that chap has, as fertile as ever."

"Every idea a winner," Thetis agreed. She undid the cuff. "You'll do."

My father and I discussed Pedro's Midas touch as we walked up the hill. My father said, "Pedro doesn't take the money seriously. It's fairy gold to him."

"What will happen to it all?"

"No idea. I don't think they have much family left."

"Don't they think of moving somewhere more comfortable? This climate can't do Freya's arthritis any good."

"They feel about Forway as I do," my father told me. "There is nowhere better. Plenty of good uses for their money here, come to think of it." He began to enumerate the comforts that Pedro's wealth could acquire for Forway. But he ended morosely, "Shouldn't be surprised if he leaves the lot to a cats' home in the end."

Pedro's oak was still sported. I said, "We had better not disturb him."

"I suppose you are right." But from farther up the hill, I noticed that the line that took power from the electricity generator to the laboratory was flapping across the ground.

"Is that Pedro's power line down?" I said.

"Very likely after the weather we have had. I think we had better just see . . ." My father returned to the closed outer door of the laboratory, a low concrete building with a green painted corrugated shed. It looked more like a cow shed than the birthplace of great invention. My father sacrilegiously knocked.

"Are you sure . . . if he's working—?" I said nervously. When Ian and I were boys, disturbing Pedro was the major crime.

My father edged his way round the side of the shed, placing his feet in the narrow gully that was supposed to prevent the accumulated water from seeping under the walls. "Just have a look to make sure."

I followed rather reluctantly. Although my father reached the small window before me, my eyes are sharper, so that we saw simultaneously through the dirty panes that Pedro's body was twisted awkwardly in collapse across the work-bench. I knew he was dead before we forced our way in through the doors.

Once we were in the room, the smell made it very apparent that Pedro had been dead for some days. It was very cold, since the electric fire must have failed when the power line came down.

Among Dr. Thetis Lisle's numerous accomplishments was a knowledge of pathology. She was able to establish that the direct cause of Pedro's death had been hypothermia. But by the time that her husband, Godfrey Lisle, acting as coroner, signed the burial certificate (before he officiated at the funeral in his role of Island Captain), everybody on the island understood how the appalling accident had happened.

Pedro's habit had been to sit at his work-bench on a high wooden stool. When he got to his feet, as he frequently did, especially when talking to people, for he had retained his Socratic teacher's habit of pacing up and down in conversation, he would push himself up in the manner of most old people, taking the weight on his wrists, with the palms of his hands flat on the work-bench in front of him.

What had he been doing? None of the scribbled papers lying around the room meant anything to those of us who tried to see whether a magically profitable formula was waiting to be patented. He would have been making something, since he never sat idle. Several half-completed models were scattered about the room, of boats and houses and machinery. The Barnes's own house, and the island's schoolroom, was full of Pedro's accurate miniatures.

He had ready to hand a tube of "super glue," that contact adhesive that so often sends model makers to the hospital with their fingers stuck together. Apparently Pedro had inadvertently spilt some of this transparent substance on his work-bench. When he put his hands down flat to rise from his stool, he was caught like a limed bird. When the electricity went off during the storm, he froze to death, there where he was stuck.

I heard one of the Yetts women, who had done a postal course on psychology, talking about death wishes and the loss of the will to live.

Sergeant Hicks, who combined the roles of coastguard, customs officer, and policeman, said that the tests had shown no alien fingerprints on the tube of glue. There was no sign that an outsider had entered the lab. Foul play was not suspected.

"But Pedro Barnes was always so scrupulously careful," my father said. Mrs. Yetts started on again about suppressed desires to end it all. Annie Windows, who had been helping Freya do housework when she was laid up with her arthritis, remarked that the house had always had an awful lot of things lying around.

"No way of making her husband tidy after all these years, Mrs. Barnes would say."

"If only one of us had noticed that he was in need of help," Thetis Lisle said mournfully. "I feel dreadfully guilty about it. I went past the place while he must have been struggling in there, and with the door closed I thought . . ."

"So did I," my father muttered.

"Did you go and see him, Mr. Gerson?" Thetis Lisle asked. "Before he closed the outer door?"

"Yes, he was very friendly to us," Rik Gerson said, and his wife nodded vigorously, "but when we went again the door was closed."

"How did you know what that meant?"

"He warned us, that first time. Said we shouldn't knock if he left it shut. So we didn't."

"There's no need for anyone to feel guilty," I said. "Pedro was of sound mind. If he sported his oak, he knew nobody would come."

"Did you notice the container of glue on his desk?" Sergeant Hicks asked Rik Gerson.

"Yes, I did. And I heard the electric generator chugging away. He had a cosy fug going in there. Snug as a bug in a rug, I thought."

Nobody else had been near the Barnes place during the storm at all.

I was to leave the day after the funeral. "What do you think Freya will do now?" I asked my father.

"She will be rich enough to do exactly as she pleases."

"What is there left to please her, with Ian and Pedro both gone?"

My father's voice sounded a little evasive. "I shall help her as best I can. We are very old friends."

The idea floated into my mind that these two old friends might marry and end their days together, but I said nothing of that when I bade my father goodbye. The Gersons were travelling back in the helicopter too, having arranged to take possession of the Aragon farm in June, and Godfrey Lisle was coming too. Thetis had decided he should go to be with Freya.

WITH NO KNOWN STARTING POINT, Tamara had to begin her work, of both kinds, at random. Her curiosity had been aroused by talk of Mrs. Anholt's Irish lodger at The Castle. She had been trained to follow random scents when the course of an investigation was vague; in any case, there was an ineradicable connection in her mind between her undercover trade and the Irish.

Tamara walked from Freya's cottage towards Trinder's Island—an island in name only, except at high tide, or when there was a strong north-west wind; otherwise, there was a causeway formed by a bar of shingle that led to the three-acre mound of heather and bracken. The old man who had caused The Castle to be built had planned to raise the causeway and have it surfaced but in the end enjoyed his isolation too much to do so.

Continuous barking could be heard from The Castle. Unimaginative though she liked to think herself, Tamara felt a prickle of illogical fear down her spine. She swung her ranging-pole jauntily and hitched her field-bag more firmly across her shoulder. As far as anyone else was concerned, this expedition was both innocent and licit. To prove it, she made first for Trinder's Barrow, a long low mound at the top of the hill. The hillside was peaty and her feet sunk into the sweet-smelling ooze, but the barrow itself was dry, and

Tamara unhitched her equipment and lay down on the ground.

She was at the highest point of the western cliffs. To her right was the ravine that separated Trinder's Island from the rest of Forway; behind, the mossy damp hillside gradually shaded to the marginally richer fields near The Town; in front of her, four hundred feet of sedimentary rocks fell to a boiling sea. The cliff side was tufted with grass and whitened by bird droppings, but the general impression was dark and lowering. It was hard to believe that until quite recently islanders would let themselves down from here to collect eggs, as the Faeroes islanders were said still to do.

Trinder's Barrow was falling into the sea. Tamara edged forward on her stomach to peer over the eroded edge. Ian Barnes's notes, made when he was still a schoolboy, mentioned that he had found some sherds, later identified as Bronze Age, sticking from the section of earth.

Tamara was absorbed by archaeological fascination when she felt a nip on her left buttock. With a presence of mind an assailant had no right to expect she jerked backward, not forward over the cliff, before rolling over and sitting up. She stared furiously at the man who was standing above her.

"You see that I couldn't resist it," he said.

"You are bloody lucky you didn't kill me," Tamara answered and got up to find that her eyes were level with his. A small man, then, bearded, and wearing clothes that were tattered even by the standards of Forway. "You must be Mr. Gerson," she said coldly.

"That's right, pleased to meet you. Miss Tamara Hoyland, from the smoke, isn't it?" he said, holding out a very dirty hand. She shook it unenthusiastically. "Wonderful up here, isn't it?" he went on, sweeping the horizon with a huge pair of field-glasses. He took a notebook from his back-pack. "I always note down unusual birds," he said.

Tamara looked through her own very powerful minia-ture binoculars. "Those are only shags," she said.

"I was looking farther out."

There were no birds to be seen farther out and Mr. Gerson did not seem interested in the fulmar that sailed in and out of the cliff; but on the horizon, ships of various sizes could be seen all around the island, and the horizon was cas-tellated by tankers. Tamara had a disquieting vision of ships circling Forway like sharks around a sinking ship.

Rik Gerson squatted down on the barrow. "Dandelion coffee?" Tamara shook her head and drew out her own flask of caffeine-laden liquid. She had never much liked the peo-ple of her own generation who dropped out of society, and like a Tory die-hard, which otherwise she was not, she resented the proportion of her earnings that was taxed to support them. A pair of ravens were calling and swooping near the cliff top, but Rik Gerson ignored them, and Tamara swung her binoculars round to survey the rest of Trinder's Island. From this vantage point The Castle was supremely apparent, a statement of neurosis and *folie de grandeur* on a massive scale. The side visible from the main island, and from passing ships, was a long crenellated wall built of the ugly local stone, with a few ill-proportioned windows all covered with rusty iron grilles. This frontage was attached to a disproportionately small house, fully visi-ble only from the hill above. Behind it a yard was littered with rubbish, and two large dogs were leaping and tugging at their chains.

"Funny you should come to Forway just now," Rik Gerson remarked. He scratched his knee through a tear in his jeans and then withdrew his bloody finger to suck it.

Tamara looked away and said, "Early summer is the usual time for archaeological field-work."

"I meant The Visit. And U.D.I. And all that."

"I don't see why it should affect me."

"You didn't know about it before you left London?" he asked, peering too closely into her face.

"No."

"I thought, seeing as you are a civil servant . . ."

"I don't know what you mean," Tamara said stiffly. "I'm on the staff of the Royal Commission for Ancient and Historical Monuments."

"So I heard," he said meaningfully. "We've all heard about you." His dirty hand moved towards Tamara's. She began to put her binoculars into their case.

She said, "And do you support the independence for Forway?"

"Yeah—why not? If it makes them happy."

"You don't feel that it's dangerous?"

"In what way?"

"Giving a stepping-stone to some foreign power?"

"Doesn't matter to me. I don't care about things like nationalities. They are all the same. Like the Forway men— what has the U.K. ever done for me, that's what I'd like to know."

"You don't feel patriotic?"

"Why should I? All that stuff about loyalty, all the flag-waving . . . they used to talk about it in my work. Public employees, they called us, as though it made a difference to the job. I did it okay, because they paid me, as simple as that. The ideology is just eyewash."

Tamara stood up.

"I must get on. There probably won't be many days when the weather is clear." Even now, heavy clouds were scudding across from the west, and in the distance a broad grey strip dropping to the sea showed where the rain was already falling.

"Can I help?" he said. "I know about digs. I've had friends who went digging." The tone of his voice implied a double meaning.

Tamara replied blandly, "At the university, do you mean?"

"When I was in the Civil Service—just like you. Until I was disabled. Luckily there was an insurance scheme on special Civil Service terms. That's how we could afford to come here." He picked up the end of the measuring tape, but Tamara took it from him.

"It's a one-woman job," she said. She carried on measuring and drawing while he marched down the hill and across the causeway. Once he was out of sight, she went on scanning Trinder's Castle. Nothing could be seen to move there but the dogs, and she had got down to the eastern beach below the less grandiose side wall and was eating her sandwiches when she first heard human sounds from inside.

The voice was just like that of the late Mike or the late Rory. The hairs on her head prickled. For the first time since that decisively murderous evening, Tamara felt, not so much guilty, as fully aware of what she had done.

"Don't you be forgetting now," the voice said. "You're to be there to meet her. Nine o'clock and don't fail."

"I won't, Frank, you know I won't."

"And that's just to remind you." The sound of a slap. The man came round onto the beach, an ordinary-looking man with dark hair and palish skin. He began to pull a dinghy down the beach towards the water. He did not notice Tamara, who was lying concealed by a shingle bank. She watched as he launched the boat and climbed into it. He began to row straight out to sea, and Tamara realized that he was making for a large fishing boat, one of the kind that is festooned with the radio equipment that makes a mockery of the word *wireless*. She did not wait until he had climbed aboard but made her way around The Castle walls to the yard. The dogs were still barking madly, but when Tamara appeared they increased their noise to a crazy ululation, and Nonie Anholt came out of the back door. She shouted, though her voice was inaudible over the din, and soon went inside again to fetch something that she threw to the animals from a safe distance. They began to gulp the food, and Mrs. Anholt came over to Tamara.

"Who are you?"

Tamara introduced herself. "Marvellous, do come in." Mrs. Anholt's voice was that of a much younger woman. "Come and see The Castle properly. You'll appreciate it." Tamara followed her through the back door into a smelly lobby. She glanced automatically at her reflection in a fly-spotted glass that hung crooked on the wall, and straightened her hair. "Ah, you're still at that stage," Mrs. Anholt remarked. "I have become perfectly indifferent to my appearance. It's like being reborn. Such freedom. I don't give a damn any more."

"Really?" Tamara murmured.

"Once I devoted my whole life to it. Brushing and curling and dyeing and plucking. I spent hours putting on paint and taking it off and being massaged or pommelled or combed. I thought I owed it to myself. My baby had hardly been born when I asked the nurse for my compact. And then suddenly one day I stopped. Just like that. I became a different person. And now I simply couldn't care less. It's so convenient that old women don't sweat. But I suppose you are still at the stage of caring."

"I don't wear much make-up."

"Natural or paint, the effect is the same if you're good at it. I should know. But nowadays I see the wrinkles and all the horrors, and they don't affect me at all. I just don't react."

Tamara understood about not reacting; she felt no reaction, emotionally, to her memory of Mike and Rory alive or how they died, though the sound of Frank's voice had reminded her of them. "Non-judgemental," she murmured.

"That's the word. That's how I feel about everything that once seemed to matter so much. You should have seen my little house in London. Convenient for Harrods and always full of flowers and magazines and pretty little touches. Hours of my life, years, I spent on that. All over."

That no time was spent on this house was self-evident. Great festoons of cobwebs hung down from every corner, and every flat surface was covered with greasy dust. There were graveyards of flies on the window sills. Tamara followed into what might once have been a library. There were still a few mildewed books on the shelves, but most were bare or had on them such things as empty bottles, dirty plates, and cigarette stubs.

"Have you lived here for a long time, Mrs. Anholt?"

Nonie Anholt sat down on a sagging-springed sofa, releasing a cloud of dust, and drew her feet up under her skirt. "I'll tell you all about it," she promised. "Come and sit down. Frank's away for the night, there's no worry."

"Frank?"

"Don't be silly, you have heard all about him. I saw you with Freya Barnes and those chatterboxes in The Town. She's going senile since Pedro went. Helped on his way, Frank says, don't know who by though. Don't tell me you haven't heard about the violent Irishman who lives up here? They wrote to my son, Peter, about it in Surrey. Lucikly he is too busy to come and interfere. He finds me very embarrassing. In his world people live as though they were about to be photographed for *Ideal Home Magazine*. Peter wrote that I should consider how my life-style would shame them if their friends knew about me. No doubt they'd stick social workers onto me, if there were any here. What nobody seems to understand is that I like living like this. I won't say that I actually relish being knocked about, no doubt you have noticed the bruises, but I like having a young man to keep me company and I like living as I choose."

"Frank's your lodger, is he?"

"You could call him that." The expression of a much younger, sexually successful woman surfaced and sank among the wrinkles, and Tamara understood what made Nonie Anholt accept the battering. Perhaps it even turned her on; Rory had got his kicks from administering blows, and on the only occasion he tried it on Tamara, she had realized that there were women who would have revelled in it. "Anyway," Mrs. Anholt added, "I like to hear the brogue around this house again."

"Again?"

"My first fiancé was an Irishman. Look." She blew the dust off a framed photograph. It showed a blank-faced young man in striped tie and a boating jacket, with a straw hat on the back of his head.

"Was he killed in the war?"

"You could call it that. Killed is just what he was. But I'll pay them out . . ."

"Did he live here too then?"

"He was my cousin. When he left it was like a light being turned out. I left too, of course. I joined up, and then I wasn't back here for years, I didn't come until my grandfather's funeral, and by then my mother and father and brother were all dead too, and I'd been engaged more times than I can remember, and married twice. But it stays with you, you'll find that out. Nothing is ever so real again as your first love affair."

Tamara made a grim, silent promise to Ian's ghost: I shan't end like this. Aloud she said, "What happened on Forway during the war? Did the Germans attack it?"

"No. I don't think anyone took much notice here. After all, they were neutral in the Republic, weren't they?"

"You don't think there's too much patriotism in Forway then?"

"Patriotism? For which country? We're no more British than we're Irish. All my mother's family came from Donegal, anyway. Do you want to look around this pile? My grandfather was one of the few Forway men who left to make a fortune and came back to spend it here. This is his visible expression of success."

And so it might have been, once; everything was too derelict now to seem like anything except failure. Collapse and squalor lay all around, but Nonie Anholt glanced about her complacently and said, "Isn't everything messy? My mamma would have had a fit. I dare say I would have once upon a time. I tell you what I've done, Tamara Hoyland. I've come out of my cupboard, isn't that the fashionable phrase? I live how I choose, and nobody can stop me, and I don't care what anyone thinks any more. If that isn't independence, tell me what is."

✳

ON THE DAY TAMARA WENT TO FORWAY, I too was on my way there. I was on a boat called the *Eurydice*, circumnavigating the British Isles. My role was to lecture to the paying passengers about the literary associations of our various landfalls. I had used the preparing of my three lectures as an excuse for not writing the book I was under contract to produce; I had spent far too long doing research, like an undergraduate with an overdue essay, so that a pile of neat notes would make me think the day well spent. But all the time I knew that I should be doing other work. I left my desk ready for a new start, a fresh ream of paper, a new ribbon in the typewriter, and a new file waiting for the completed pages, and as I shut my front door I told myself that I would return invigorated after two weeks at sea and a week on Forway.

I felt the relief of a released prisoner when I left the flat in which my previous months had been so unproductive. Guilt is the natural condition of the free-lance writer, as the headmaster warned me when I left a secure teaching post to become one, but it was not always as justified as mine that day. Guilt and dread; for the prospect of two weeks enclosed in a ship with two hundred strangers was daunting too.

The other passengers looked unpromising at first sight,

nearly all elderly and mostly American. The other lecturers were a landscape gardener, a clergyman, and the archaeologist Thea Crawford. On embarkation at Southampton we eyed each other with the hostility of the British forced to be matey with strangers, and the mateyness of strangers forced into intimacy by their work. By York we were on first-name terms; by Edinburgh we had become well enough acquainted to go off together for the day while everyone else went to buy their quota of tartan.

I wanted to see Orkney and Shetland, though; I had originally accepted the invitation because ordinary life would not take me there. Thea Crawford and I were in the front of the queue for the launches that were to ferry us across to Dingwall. We had reached the stage of giggling together—lecturers allied against the rest—and Thea whispered scurrilous suggestions about the private lives of inoffensive lawyers from America's eastern seaboard.

"And there's one I swear I have never seen before," she said.

"You'll still be saying that when we disembark at Southampton," one of the cruise organizers told her.

"Do you mean one never learns to tell the difference between them?" I asked, running my eye over the rows of identical burberries. I had already noticed that there were several apparently indistinguishable pairs of men and women on board, for I had sat next to two of them on successive evenings, and the second conversation, not surprisingly, had led to some embarrassment. But that was not what the girl meant.

"There are always pairs like twins, every trip. But you do get to recognize people you have had a bit of a chat with. But there are some people who don't turn up for the bus tours or meals or the lectures—"

"And half those who do sleep through them," I said.

"If they don't come and change their currency, or ask for the doctor, or anything like that—well, there are some we just never see."

There were not many faces in the crowd that I could recognize, but I had been lying a little low myself, not feeling exactly sick but rather as though I were about to feel sick any minute. The collected passengers gave a disconcertingly homogeneous impression. I reminded myself severely that each was an individual with a unique life history and personality. The cruise organizers referred to passengers in bulk as "pax." I warned myself against herding them into a collective noun in my own mind.

That one, for instance: an elderly woman with a younger companion. Perhaps the girl would be good value, if one had a chance to talk to her; short nails, neatly kept—a musician, perhaps, or a surgeon? But I knew that she was more likely a typist or computer operator. She wore a bulky sweater anorak, dark glasses, woolly hat, effectively hiding her figure and face. There was more personality apparent in the older woman, who was not dressed in the uniform of the matrons on board, who queued to have their hair set every day by a sad-looking hairdresser, and who wore toning tweeds and knits, bangles, and tactfully knotted scarves. This woman wore a long woven skirt, tennis shoes, and a fisherman's jersey and looked sensible but eccentric. I decided to aim for this pair's table at lunch or dinner; but the cruise organizer was right, for I did not see them again that day, or the next, on Shetland, or the one after that, in the outer Hebrides.

By then one was resigned to life on board, to the international food, the sultry, sweaty heat of the airless cabins, the gloom of the Greek crew as their ship sailed farther on into inhospitable northern waters. The lump of passengers began to break down into individuals; I met a retired explorer from Nova Scotia, a retired nurse from the Australian outback, and a shy pseudonymous writer of considerably more fame than myself. I was polite about where I got my ideas from at the lunch table and about whether I type or handwrite at dinner. I spoke to somnolent audiences about Boswell and Johnson, and Somerville and Ross. I listened to Professor Thea Crawford lecturing about Scottish prehistory, to the young woman from Kew Gardens about the gardens at Inverewe and Garnish, to the chaplain about the gathering of the clans and Irish nationalism. By the time we docked at Galway I watched the passengers stream down the gangplank to the waiting coaches with some relief that I was to have a day in my own company. Being whizzed round Connemara by a driver who would be unlikely to glance at the road more than once a minute was not my idea of fun. I planned to spend a happy day in the rabbit warren of Kenny's antiquarian bookshop.

The intellectual-looking old woman, on whom I had not set eyes since the Orkneys, had evidently also decided to skip the scenic tour. Clutching the arm of her companion she edged down the gangway to the quay. The younger woman was swaddled like an Eskimo again. I noticed her glance at the granite wall of the warehouse nearby, which had an enormous message sprayed onto it in red paint: "Brits out." But a poster nearby read, "Ireland of the Welcomes." Beside that was a row of identical small posters, showing one of those unrecognizable police photographs of wanted criminals: a female escaped prisoner, on the "most wanted" list.

The wind had been strong all down the west of Ireland —a good many of the tourists were greenly wan that morning at breakfast—and a sudden gust blew off the younger woman's hat. She jumped for it, her black hair blowing out behind her, and for a moment her prominent black eyes met mine. I watched the two women walk off into the town.

I was back on the deck by the end of the day to watch all the passengers return. Thea Crawford had brought a friend and his family on board for a drink, an archaeologist from Galway, whose children rampaged happily about the usually sedate decks. Thea told him about her family: a son, with the appalling name of Clovis, who was on an expedition studying endemic diseases in South America, and her husband, the journalist Sylvester Crawford, who was writing a book about prison conditions in the Third World. Not long before, he had been in a Turkish gaol, wrongly suspected of drug smuggling, and naturally had chosen that subject for his next crusade. I had known that this elegant academic woman was married to a famous reforming journalist, but she was deeply ignorant of current affairs herself, and it did seem a strange match.

After the busses had unloaded their weary passengers, a few stragglers returned to the ship late. We watched the keen photographer from Utah, who had spent the day adding to her collection of twelve thousand slides; my fellow writer, whom I had seen earlier in the day in Kenny's, almost delirious, and who now returned to the ship in a taxi and needed help to carry the three cratesful of books he had bought; the two women I had seen that morning. They came in a battered car and scuttled up the gangway just in time, for the customs officer and the archaeologist had left, and we sailed immediately.

I delivered my own final lecture that evening and then stayed on in the lounge to listen to the chaplain talking about Forway. Of course I already knew most of what he said, but I had to admire the way he made dry detail interesting to uninformed holiday-makers.

Forway, he explained, was neither autonomous as the

Isle of Man and the Channel Islands were, with independent legislature and governor, nor was it properly a part of
the United Kingdom like the Isles of Scilly and the Hebrides.

"The trouble is, it has been convenient for governments
to forget it," he said. "A few more niggles from lawyers in
the past would have—for once—been no bad thing. Now,
take the Scillies: their name is always included in any stat-
ute. Not Forway's though; but it is never formally excluded
either. Or what about tax? Well, the Scillonians started to
pay income tax in 1953 and road fund licences even later.
On Forway, nobody has ever earned enough to pay income
tax and there aren't any roads. The Health Service doesn't
run a hospital there. The ferry to Cork is quicker than the
ferry to Penzance, so islanders tend to go to the Republic
for treatment. There's a primary school, and some of the
children have gone as boarders for secondary education in
Cornwall; but quite a few just didn't get any other school-
ing. There's no public library: they don't pay rates, just a
small sum they call tithes, which supports such services as
they do have. Nobody has ever formally said which diocese
of the Church it's in. Sometimes they have a priest from Ireland, sometimes they are sent a curate from Cornwall,
sometimes the chaplain of the Isles of Scilly pays a visit. But
their marriages are celebrated as though they were on a
ship at sea—their boss, their mayor—actually they call him
the captain—performs the marriages, and nobody has ever
got round to testing their legality. Probably the whole population is illegitimate.

"As you'll see when we land there tomorrow, it's a fear-
fully desolate spot. Before helicopters were invented, people
could be waiting for weeks for the sea to calm enough to
land or embark at Forway. Even on what seemed to be a
calm day, a sudden storm might push the sea into waves

forty feet high, and until a rudimentary jetty was built by the navvies in the first war, landings from the boats had to be made onto slippery rock. It's a miracle it's survived as an inhabited island. You'd have thought it would be evacuated, as St. Kilda was in the thirties. But of course, one of St. Kilda's problems was the decline in population. The poor brutes had been killing their own babies by smearing gunk tainted with tetanus on the cord at birth. Forway was saved from that kind of tragedy by a Scotswoman who moved there in the eighteen eighties. She and her husband reorganized them and ever since then they have managed somehow. It's a remarkable story, what the Lisles did for Forway.

"But nobody even knows who the place belongs to. There doesn't seem to be a landowner, and nobody who owes allegiance to the Crown. The Scillies belong to the Duke of Cornwall, that is, to the Crown. The Hebrides all belong to Scottish landowners, or they did, until bits were sold off to rich Dutchmen and Arabs. But Forway—nobody is sure. Nobody seems to be responsible, and until recently nobody had worried. The idea seems to be that they once belonged to the Dukes of Brittany, then they belonged to an Irish grandee . . . but after about A.D. 1500, unspecified. Three sovereign states have claimed it, and there's to be a case heard at the International Court at The Hague, between France, the United Kingdom, and Eire. Perhaps they'll ask us for our passports tomorrow."

I talked to the chaplain afterwards and said, "But of course it is part of the United Kingdom—must be. After all, I was born there and I've got a British passport. There's a police sergeant, and he certainly has a uniform, even if he doesn't wear it.

"That's evidence of custom and practice, of course. But you never know with these supra-national courts—The

Hague, Strasbourg, Luxembourg. They sometimes make the most bizarre judgements. You may yet turn out to be an Irishman or a Breton, my dear chap."

I got landed with the ship's bore at dinner and felt very sour afterwards as I watched the Greek chanteuse, who spent her days in some nameless bowels of the ship, singing repetitive songs. I watched dapper old gentlemen steering well-upholstered ladies around the tiny circular floor, in the middle of the Atlantic Ocean, to the sound of bazouki music. I was glad that this was my last evening.

The sea had calmed a little by daybreak, which was just as well. Like the captain, I knew well the warning to mariners in *The British Islands Pilot:*

> Before approaching Forway, all vessels should be prepared to batten down, and the hatches of small vessels ought to be secured even in the finest weather, as it is difficult to see what may be going on at a distance, and the transition from smooth water to a broken sea is so sudden that no time is given for making arrangements.

Then the warning continues:

> Sometimes a sea is raised which cannot be imagined by those who have never experienced it.

As Charles Darwin had written of Tierra del Fuego, and as I could write of Forway, "The sight of such a coast is enough to make a landsman dream for a week about death, peril and shipwreck."

The *Eurydice* was narrow enough to go through the Corinth Canal, and its draught was shallow enough to approach most of the Aegean Islands, but the approach to Forway, as I have shown, is notorious, and while I stood on the bridge directing the passengers' attention to details of the view through the loudspeaker, I watched the monoglot captain gesturing his refusal to the pilot's injunctions to approach the shore more closely. I read aloud to my phlegmatic audience the words of an eighteenth-century seafarer about the stupendous cliff face on the other side of the island. "We should not have been more dismayed by an island of demons, and should have said that naught else could inhabit it but that its reputation had been made known to us before." When the ship did scrape, hardly perceptibly, against the bottom, the captain's shriek drowned both my monologue and the pilot's assurances about the making tide. The pilot was John Windows, and when he moved away to his boat he saw me.

"They all have to float off here, Magnus, you know that. There's no other way to reach Forway."

As I had been telling my audience, the island was barricaded by sharp submerged rocks. Only one narrow channel allowed ships to approach Harbour Bay, and there the water was dangerously shallow.

Too few tourists visit Forway for there to be a fleet of launches ready to ferry them off, as there is in Orkney, or Scilly. The *Eurydice*'s lifeboats were swung down to take everybody on shore. One had to admire the courage of the passengers, old, lame, and faltering but undaunted by ladders and swinging gangplanks. The old woman with her swaddled companion was handed down by some sailors with some difficulty into one of the small orange boats. I thanked whatever providence watched me that there had been no taking to the boats at midnight on this cruise.

Of course there are not tourist coaches on Forway; the day's programme was for "free exploration." I had offered to show Thea Crawford the island. We jumped into the lifeboat, with my luggage, and I caught a glance from the old woman's companion that disconcerted me mightily, but it was not until I had landed, and given my bags to one of the Yetts boys to trundle up to my father's house, that I realized why. I had thought that the younger of these two women had dark hair and eyes, but this woman had pale northern eyes with undarkened lashes. I shrugged it off: a different-coloured contact lens, a different woman, it made no difference to me, for I was shot of the *Eurydice* now and had to get into the right mood for Forway instead.

PROFESSOR CRAWFORD SAID that she had grown out of enjoying cold walks across desolate landscapes looking at evidence of the past. Seeing her narrow shoes and spotless trouser suit, I could believe it. I asked her what she would like to see instead.

"I don't know, Magnus. The essence of the place. What picture comes to your mind if you think of Forway?"

"A smell, more than a picture."

She sniffed experimentally. "No good. I've got a cold." We all had colds. I believed that the germs were distributed by the *Eurydice*'s air-conditioners. So Thea and I went into The Hotel instead. It was a small building made mostly of painted corrugated iron, yellow, with blue window frames and door. The bar was furnished with the type of metal-and-plastic furniture advertised in mail-order catalogues. Few tourists ever stayed on Forway, so that there was no need for folksiness, and though the island had once been "dry," alcohol was a major import now. Annie Foggo poured us brandy and ginger ale, although it was only ten o'clock. She said that Sergeant Hicks—not that he ever enforced the licencing laws—was away in England. "In England?" Thea asked.

"A foreign country," I said, and Annie Foggo nodded. Then two of Thea's compatriots came in begging for gin, and it turned out that Thea knew them through her husband, so there was a lot of chatter about the *Eurydice*, and where Sylvester was now, lucky sod. I had heard of Carl Hawker, naturally, but I did not admire him or his writing, though my judgement was perhaps affected by jealousy of his fame, since he was a year younger than myself. He had ridden to fame by exposing traitors in the Secret Services but somehow managed always to write about world politics and spying as though they were pornographic. I wondered what he was doing on Forway.

"What are you doing here anyway?" Thea said. "Holiday?"

"Hardly. No, there was supposed to be a story, but I haven't found it."

"What was it?" I asked, astonished. The last place on earth, I'd have thought, for a story to interest Carl Hawker.

"Nothing. There's some royal visit due, but that's not my bag at all. Met your father, though. Couldn't make out what a bloke like him does all day here."

Carl Hawker seemed interested in my father's life-style, and we chatted about that for a while. Then Maggie, the photographer, began to grumble about being marooned on Forway for another three days, and I told her to go and talk nicely to the management of the *Eurydice*, since my cabin would now be vacant. They left, promising favours to compensate me.

Thea said, "Sylvester says there is more to Carl Hawker than you think."

"More spy rings still unrevealed, you mean?"

"No, it was something about being given scoops in exchange for services rendered. I can't remember the details. I can't say I like him much, but I do quite wonder what he was doing here."

We drank some more brandy. At last I felt obliged to say, "Well, Thea, what can I show you on Forway?"

We looked at one another silently. I did not feel enthusiastic about pottering around the island in the rain. She was equally unenticed. We each knew that the other felt so, and neither of us felt able to say it. She said, "Not archaeology, anyway."

"That's just as well. I know damn all about it. I had a friend here who was keen, but he was killed in a car crash last year and I never listened to him much."

"I would quite like to see how people actually live here," Thea suggested with the air of one dredging up the only bearable possibility from a well of nastiness. "I haven't ever been anywhere quite so remote. Or should we avoid treating it like a human zoo?"

"People here used to grow rich on that." In the earlier part of the century rich yachtsmen used to come ashore at Forway to be photographed beside the huddled bothies; they paid intentionally in money, and unintentionally in infectious germs, for the privilege. Before that, benevolent societies used to be inspired by articles in such journals as the *Illustrated London News* to send comforts to these Northern Hemisphere savages. "It is less interesting now," I told Thea. "Forway men live in houses and eat convenience foods. Just like civilized Londoners."

But that, in fact, was to deny the truth that life on Forway was different from that elsewhere. The isolation itself was a differentiating factor, and the exposure to elements from which twentieth-century Europeans were protected elsewhere.

"It isn't very like the Scillies," Thea said. "I had expected . . ."

"That's partly for physical reasons. Geological differences, you know. And of course modern sensibilities regard the Scillies as beautiful. They were thought of as savage too, until people began to admire beaches and seascapes. The only holiday attraction of Forway is the 'getting away from it all' feeling. And the natives feel the opposite. If you live here you feel you can't get away, it's a very small, enclosed, inward-looking community. We all know each other's business."

"And you all know each other." All the islanders we had seen had greeted me by name and looked inquisitively at Thea. The *Eurydice*'s passengers were wandering disconsolately around the damp Town. Their scope was limited. Forway has one cluster of houses, called The Town, one road, called The Road, and one hotel, called The Hotel. The Town consists of an irregular open space, called The Square, around which stand the doctor's house, The Church, the three shops, and a scatter of cottages. Other houses are reached by footpaths that trail out into fields and hillside.

"And the Scillies are very spick and span," Thea said, kicking some litter to one side with her fastidious foot.

"The Hebrides would be a better comparison. Nobody is tidy there." Perhaps because there have been so few prosperous settlers on Forway, it has never displayed any of England's puritan cleanliness; and of course the circumstances are not favourable to gardening, so the gaunt landscape has not been disguised by burgeoning subtropical plants. The main reason, though, as in the outer Hebrides, is that Forway men are just not interested; they are deaf to the scandalized comments about mess that outsiders tend to make. The native eye is quite indifferent to the sight of empty detergent bottles, or rusty heaps of metal, or any junk abandoned where it fell.

"I usually prefer a landscape that shows the hand of man," Thea said thoughtfully. "But man's hand has hardly embellished Forway."

"It's all in the eye of the beholder." The sour, peaty landscapes of Forway were not my idea of beauty either.

How can it be that the barren hillside was not transformed when I saw Tamara Hoyland on it? She came towards us along the track where Thea and I had paused. She was slung about with canvas bags and cameras. She recognized Thea and waved to her, and they met with loud expressions of surprise and pleasure. Thea said, "Magnus, this is Tamara Hoyland. She's an archaeologist too."

"I was one of Thea's pupils; I'm doing a field survey on Forway."

I looked at her. She looked at me. And for a little while she was no more than a pretty girl, not less interesting than pretty girls always are, but not more. Was I interesting to her? I think not—not, at least, in the sense I should have liked. Her thoughts were masked by her seemingly lucid face.

"I have heard of you," I said crassly. "From Ian Barnes."

She was not offended. "I have heard of you from Ian too."

We shook hands. What did she see? A shaggy man with spirals of hair jutting from a narrow head, with a face neither bearded nor clean-shaven, with dirty finger-nails.

My own vision was blinkered. How was it possible for me to set eyes on Tamara Hoyland without realizing that my world was changed? I even felt, God help me, irritable, almost aggressive. The ground still seemed to sway under my feet, as it did on the *Eurydice*.

"Of course, I'd forgotten," Thea Crawford said. "Your boy-friend comes from Forway, doesn't he?" I tried to nudge her, or tread on her toes, but I saw Tamara Hoyland's eye on my clumsy movements, and she said quite calmly, "He did, Thea, but he's dead. Nearly a year ago now."

"My dear—I had no idea—what happened?"

"It was a motor accident. Not his fault. He was killed at once, they say."

We walked on in silence for a while, but I knew Thea Crawford well enough by now to realize that naked emotion would embarrass her, and soon she said, "Look, the boats are taking people back to the *Eurydice*. I shall leave you two to your island life." Tamara and I waited on the quay with Thea until there was room for her in a boat. We spoke of the cruise and the lectures we had given. Thea said she was glad to have circumnavigated the British Isles, once. We spoke of meeting again later in the summer, in civilization. Thea Crawford kissed Tamara goodbye and then brushed her cheek politely against my stubble. "Have fun, children," she said. We watched the boat buck across the sea to the *Eurydice*. I momentarily wished myself back in its imprisoning comfort.

"Are you going to your father's place?" Tamara said. "I'll walk with you. I am staying with Ian's mother."

I took some of her equipment from her. She walked lightly, springily, her legs moving from her hips without her bottom wiggling. She was half a head shorter than myself, and when she looked at me, her eyes met mine without messages.

I naturally invited her in for a drink when we reached my father's place. I did not like what he had done to the bothy. When he bought it from the Aragons, it had been little more than a heap of stones and mud. He had imported plasterers and paper-hangers and crates of elegant furniture. With the curtains drawn you would have thought you were in a suburb of London, except for the ineradicable smell of

Forway, presumably compounded of salt and seaweed, guano, and burning, oil-spoilt driftwood.

"I'll fetch some ice," I said. Tamara followed me into the kitchen, which was equally magnificently equipped, with American equipment humming around the walls (except when it was silenced by a generator failure) and with cantilevered glass-doored cupboards full of gleaming crocks.

"Golly," Tamara said.

"Do you like it?" I said, probably scornfully. She stood close to me, and I touched her cheek and hair with my finger. I would have done the same with any passable girl. She did not flinch and one day I would learn that she was ready to use her body as a part of her armoury. She was determined that she would kiss and I would tell, yet I felt within myself, not in her, an unusual reserve, a shyness I had not known for ten years. We were still standing there when I heard my father come into the living-room next door, and before I could go and greet him the telephone bell rang and he had lifted the receiver.

"Selwyn Paull," he barked. "Oh it's you. Yes. All according to plan. No . . . yes . . . it will obviously take a while to get under way. One of the stumbling-blocks—excuse me, I think there is someone in the house. I'll call you later. Magnus, is that you?"

"Me and Tamara Hoyland, Father."

My father came through to the kitchen. He glanced swiftly up and down Tamara's clothes, and mine, and must, I think, have assumed that we had come in from the bedrooms on the other side of the kitchen. He greeted Tamara warmly.

"Sight for sore eyes, eh Magnus? Hope I didn't disturb you."

I never knew how to answer him. All my life I had

been guilty of not living up to his expectations and angry that his expectations were so different from mine. His apparent assumption that I had been making love to Tamara was the more annoying because it was so nearly true.

FIELD-WORKING; field-walking: the laborious inspection by all means, in all ways, of an area of ground. The landscape is a palimpsest on which all man's activities have left some trace. Here a sheep-pen, there the stub of the lighthouse, erected but not maintained, replaced later on by an unmanned lightship outside Forway's rocky teeth. The materials that had built the lighthouse, like those that had formed a fish-packing station in the days when commercial success for Forway seemed possible, could now be traced to their present positions in the walls of other structures. It was a prudent recycling of materials.

Forway, Tamara thought, would amply repay an elaborate programme of field-work. Meaningful sequences of activity could be recognized among the patterns on the ground. She wished she could concentrate on archaeology now, ignoring the perverse machinations of contemporary man.

Tamara was pacing the slight undulations of a barely perceptible earthwork on Trinder's Island and hoped that another day, in evening sunlight, it might be possible to plan the oblong shadow of some now-vanished structure. Her concentration was interrupted by the pinging sounds of an electronic instrument, and she looked up to see a girl with a metal detector in her hands. Before Tamara could launch into the professional archaeologist's denunciation of that hated object, the girl flicked the switch off and called out, "Don't worry. This is just for fun, just to see whether it responds. I wouldn't dream of fossicking." A southern English voice, pleasantly cadenced. She came and squatted beside Tamara. "Some rectangular building, do you think?"

"Are you an archaeologist? Not many people would see that."

"Alas, I'm not. But I studied it once. Archaeology with history, combined honours. Our prof was very hot on field-work."

The girl's natural colouring was pale, and her skin looked dingy, as though it were a long time since she had been out of doors. Perhaps she had been ill.

"Do you live here?" Tamara asked.

"I'm just passing through. Isn't it heaven?" She lay down on the squidgy ground on her stomach and stared out towards the hazy sea. The wind ruffled her hair and clothes and she drew in deep breaths. "It's my idea of paradise."

"Not mine," Tamara said. "I like to see the sun."

"I don't care about that. It's the freedom, the loneliness . . . it's a precious place."

She could not be as young as she had seemed at first sight. There were faint lines on her forehead, and deeper grooves running downward from her nostrils showed traces of strain. "I should like to preserve it for ever." She put her face down on her folded arms and spoke with her voice muffled. "Put a glass dome over the top so that nothing ever changed. Not a blade of grass."

"So what do you think about the idea of independence?" Tamara asked, wondering whether the girl had heard of it here.

She replied, "Ach, haven't we had enough of that sort of talk in other places? I'm tired to death of it." Her face

did look as though she were tired to death, though not perhaps by that. "Let there be just one place on the globe that
we keep our murderous hands off."

Tamara went on with her work, pacing, measuring,
looking, touching. It would be worthwhile to cut a trench
across a section here. She had not had time before leaving
London to examine the aerial photographs but was sure that
they would reveal something interesting here.

The girl woke up when the rain had penetrated
through her cream-coloured Arran sweater. Tamara said,
"I'm going back." The tone of her voice implied an invitation to keep her company, but the girl said, "I think I'll stay
here a bit longer. I like to feel the rain."

"The tide's coming in. Don't forget the causeway."

"I won't." She had a sweet smile. Tamara suddenly felt
desperately lonely, remembering how she had come here
before with Ian Barnes and how they had run across the
causeway, chased by the tide, and how they had lain together on the other side, panting and embracing.

It was a relief to be distracted from these memories by
Lena Gerson's voice. She saw Tamara walking past from her
doorway and invited, almost begged, her to come in for a
cup of tea.

The Peter Aragons' farmhouse had originally been not
much more than a one-roomed shelter made of stone and
turf, with a lean-to shed for cattle at one end. The lean-to
had been converted into a kitchen and bathroom of a kind,
and the other room was both bedroom and living-room.
Like Lena Gerson's own appearance, the interior decoration
was surprising. There were few signs of self-sufficiency, no
patchwork or crochet, but furniture suitable for a young ex-
ecutive in the suburbs. Forway's damp air had not treated
those brave banners of egalitarianism kindly. Veneers were
peeling off the furniture, and the shine had left the enam-

elled "cookware." An Indian dhurra was on the hearth, where someone had pleated white paper into a fan to hide the ashes.

Lena Gerson made tea on her bottled-gas double burner and arranged cups and saucers on a glass-and-metal trolley, which she had to lift instead of wheeling across the uneven flagged floor.

"Milk and sugar? I'm afraid we can't get lemons very often here. Tell me, whereabouts in London do you work?"

"Near Piccadilly."

"Oh, do you? That's where I was. Isn't it lovely? You are lucky. I worked in a travel agency. I did so love secretarial work."

"I wonder why I never met you with Ian."

"We hardly ever saw each other, I'm afraid. I am only a second cousin once removed. Freya's great-aunt was my great-grandmother. I just saw Ian once or twice when I first came to London, that was all."

"Where is your own home?"

"I still think of London as home, but I grew up in Sheffield."

"It must seem strange living here, after those big cities."

"Yes, it does—well, what I mean is, it's lovely, so peaceful and away from it all. A real change from the hustle and bustle. No pollution. Clean air. Food we have grown ourselves. No clock watching."

Tamara had often heard the litany of arguments against evil town life, and she noticed that Lena trotted out every one as though she had once learned them off by heart.

Lena brushed some dirt off her dark blue skirt. When she moved her leg, a small hole in her nylon tights ran into a ladder. "I am always snagging my tights on things," she complained. "It is so difficult to keep your things nice here."

"Yes, it must be," Tamara said. She had not brought a skirt or tights with her to Forway.

"I got this skirt at Fortnum and Mason, in a sale," Lena said. "Christmas before last. I bet there's lovely things in there now. I used to go and look in my lunch-hour."

"Freya told me you make things from your own spinning and so on," Tamara said. "I should love to see."

"Come and look. I'll show you." Lena opened the door and jumped back with a gasp. A dead shrew had been deposited on the step. "That cat! Rik's not here. He's gone to collect driftwood for the fire." She looked about her helplessly.

"Shall I deal with it?"

"Oh, I couldn't expect you . . . somehow I can't bring myself to touch them. It's always happening. If Rik's here—"

Tamara picked up the shrew and threw it into a mess of brambles at the edge of the yard.

"I know it's ever so silly of me. You are brave. I can't seem to get over feeling . . ." Lena's voice trailed away.

"It must be rather inconvenient living here, if you feel like that."

"Oh, yes, it is. I'm always nervous when I open doors, what I'll find on the other side. It's so stupid. Rik says that any spot of turbulence he can always deal with. Still, if you are here . . ." She pulled open a battered door into a collapsing shed. Making and mending their property was evidently not one of Rik's priorities. "There's the wool for spinning." A shapeless heap of unspun wool was heaped into a cardboard box, exuding its powerful smell. Some cans of paint stood beside it, with a messy heap of driftwood piled against the wall, and a small hand-operated printing-press on the table. "You don't get much heat from a fire made with peat, we find," Lena explained. A confused cackling noise could be heard through the back wall of the shed, mingled with excited barking. "Oh goodness, that's the geese. Oh dear. I suppose Rik isn't back yet. I'd better just see . . ."

Left alone, Tamara had a speedy look in and under things. A brown parcel beside the printing-press contained copies of the notice about Forway's Declaration of Independence, of which Mr. Black had shown her a copy. Some rolls of plastic insulating foam lay against the wall, and one escaped to lie beside the heap of wool. A variety of carpentry tools, some of them very rusty, were heaped on the table. Under a tattered and grimy manual called *How to Succeed at Cultivating Mushrooms* was a gold propelling pencil, engraved with the initial B. Ian had possessed a pencil just like that, and Tamara remembered that Lena had been his cousin. It was a desirable little object, with elaborate flowers chased down its shaft, and Tamara weighed its heaviness longingly in her hand. How many times had its twin lain on the dressing-table beside Ian's wallet, heap of small change, and bunch of keys. If it had not been worth quite a lot of money, she would have put it in her pocket for remembrance. Nothing on or of Ian's person had survived the explosion in which he died. When Lena came back, Tamara was holding some of the wool, gently tugging and twisting.

"I can't think how you turn this into knitting wool."

"It's a knack." Lena bent to pick up the roll of foam. "This is for insulation."

"You have to be careful if you cook on gas, don't you?"

"Our problem is too much ventilation here, not too little." Out in the yard, Tamara asked whether the geese were all right. "Yes, thank goodness. I'm terrified of having to deal with them. It was one of the boys from The Town, with his dog, but luckily he called it off."

"I must go back. Freya will be expecting me. How do you think she is coping?"

"I do what I can," Lena said.

"It is very good of you."

"She is a bit vague, though. She loses her way and forgets what she is talking about. Rik says she isn't all there. He doubts whether she is of sound mind, but I think that's going a bit far. It can't help being lonely for the poor old thing. And Ian dying like that must have aged her. It must give her a queer turn every time she sees that man Mrs. Anholt's got at The Castle."

"What do you mean?"

"Well, you know. Thinking about those IRA bombers and that."

"Did Freya tell you about how Ian died?" Tamara asked. Lena looked startled.

She said, "Yes. Yes, of course she did. When we came to live here, Rik and I."

"I can't help feeling that it was your husband who chose to move to the country. Was he brought up in a place like this?"

"Not to say quite like this, no. He comes from Lincolnshire."

"Perhaps his family were self-sufficient, though," Tamara suggested.

"Oh, no. Rik's father worked for the post office."

"So public service ran in the family, then. Wasn't Rik in the Civil Service?"

"Oh yes, but that was quite different," Lena said, conscious of her husband's exalted status. "Rik went to grammar school and university. He was at Leicester, he studied Law. Rik's very clever, you know."

"I wonder why he chose to go into the Civil Service."

"He had thought of being a barrister, actually. But it

was ever so difficult to get into chambers. And then some man came to Leicester recruiting for the Civil Service. So he did that instead."

"Which department was he in?" Tamara asked.

"He moved around a bit. When I met him it was the Department of Health and Social Security. The pay was good, but it meant being away from home every so often. He had to go round looking at hospitals and things."

"That doesn't sound a very dangerous trade," Tamara said. "How did he get injured?"

"It was an accident on a building site. Something fell on his head and he was concussed. There's nothing to show now, of course, but he couldn't remember things. You know what I mean, he kept forgetting things, which wasn't much good in that job. So they invalided him out."

"But what made you choose to live on Forway? Was it just because of your cousin Freya?"

"Oh no. Nothing like that. That wasn't anything to do with it. We just wanted to get away from it all. Leave all our cares as far behind us as we could." Lena's laugh was silvery and sounded slightly inane. She stood where there should be, and might once have been, a gate, as Tamara went along the path from the Aragons' old place. When Tamara looked back, Lena was still standing there, but it was only as Tamara turned that the expression on her face changed from anxiety to a brilliant smile, so that the departing guest should retain the image of a woman happy in her work and play, happy, happy, every day.

"THERE WILL BE A LEADER, a visionary and a front man," Mr. Black had said. "One to think it up, one to work out how to swing it, and a third to take the blame."

When I turned up on Forway, Tamara Hoyland wondered whether, or where, I fitted into that pattern; she was already sure that my father, Selwyn Paull, was deeply involved, both publicly and in secret.

Tamara was there, in Freya's house, while old conspirators revealed their deep-laid plans to me, and showed me all their files full of details, and prepared statements, arranged in a walnut bureau—Queen Anne, full of little drawers and cupboards, and badly warped by Forway's climate. I said, "You are in your dotage, the pair of you. You and my father, Freya. Even if you are an innocent at large, he isn't. He's just trying to see if the old hand has lost its cunning. He ought to be certified."

Freya's hands did not even pause in their knitting. "Why is that, dear?"

"For God's sake. We can't let Forway go. In the world of real politics and real money—"

"We?"

"Britain. The United Kingdom. Damn it, Father—"

"Don't you feel like a Forway man then?" Freya asked.

"Certainly I do. A Briton from Forway."

"You would have been a Frenchman from Forway, if a

mediaeval Duke of Brittany had not betted too much on a falcon."

"Or an Irishman from Forway, if old Devalera had read the small print."

"History, twistery," I snapped.

"Not a bit of it. You know quite well that both France and Ireland dispute Britain's title to Forway," my father said.

"That's one of the reasons H.M. Government have given for refusing to invest capital here," Freya said.

"Nobody cares about all that now," I told them. "Gamble with Forway in the nineteen eighties, and it will be scooped straight into Russia's lap. You wouldn't like that."

"I doubt if that would be allowed," Freya said, still with that idiotic serenity.

"You mean," I said through gritted teeth, "that you want to be protected by the Western Alliance without owing it any loyalty."

"No, we don't want to be protected or attacked. We just want to be left alone."

I said, "How can you imagine that a place is not British when there is an English policeman stationed here?"

"Oh dear. Sergeant Hicks," Freya said. "I feel quite guilty about him. You know he was ill after having a meal with me. Such a nice man too, I really don't know what I can have done to the food. I know I'm growing very absent-minded."

"Weren't you ill too?" I asked.

"Not at all."

My father interrupted, still on the former track. "After all, if they send the whole British navy to the South Atlantic to protect the right of a few Falkland Islanders to self-determination, they can hardly send even one ship here to deprive us of ours."

I watched Freya's old hands twinkling as she knitted.
Forway women had learned to knit from a Shetlander
brought there for a winter by Godfrey Lisle's redoubtable
grandmother, and now, like Shetlanders, Forway women
knitted almost faster than the eye could follow. Once a film
of Shetlanders' knitting had been laughed off a cinema
screen in London because the audience wrongly supposed
that it had been speeded up. I groaned and got up to take
some whisky. I needed it.

"You are an innocent, Freya. And Father is a fool."

"Why don't you leave us to our foolishness, dear boy,"
Freya said indulgently. "Take Tamara for a drive in the
Frog."

"I checked the fan belt for you, Freya," my father told
her.

"Oh good. Actually, I had it in at Yetts's this morning.
But that means it's fine for you to take, children. Off you
go." They were in their dotage, as I had told them. I just
hoped they would not be able to make any real mischief,
those two old things plotting their schemes together.

"Where shall we go?" I asked Tamara.

"Don't mind. Wherever you like."

I sat with my hands on the wheel, thinking about the
two people inside the house. "It's easy enough to see what
my father is up to. He's a retired administrator leaping at
the chance to do some admin. again. Everything tidy and
neat about him, that's what he likes. The organization man.
I shouldn't think he gives a damn for their airy fairy aspira-
tions. He just enjoys making sure they do everything properly."

"You know best," Tamara said. "But there is quite a lot
of scope for making trouble here, I'd have thought. It would
be very much in the interest of some foreign powers to get

their clutches on Forway, what with the oil and the territorial waters and the shipping lanes."

"How right you are. That's what I was trying to get Freya and my father to understand. Old, deluded, arteriosclerotic . . ."

"Is your father a native of Forway?"

I started the engine, and we bumped off over the hillside. "No, it was my mother who came from here. They met during the war when he was stationed in the garrison, and afterwards he took her away to govern the empire."

"So you must be related to all those Aragons and Yetts and Windows—"

"And Foggos and Lisles," I finished the litany for her. "Actually, no. My grandfather was a Dutchman who settled here hoping to make a fortune out of herrings. He didn't, of course. I really don't know why my father came back here when he retired. My mother died when I was small. Not that he has roots anywhere else; his own people were Indian Civil Service."

"Do you not think of Forway as home, then?"

I did not. To me, I said, Forway was no more than a pleasant place to come for the holidays. That was not entirely true, but I did not yet know that Tamara was a person with whom I should be truthful. I knew that she must have preconceptions about me. I had known Ian Barnes intimately, though for most of our lives more as a close enemy than a close friend. We were thrown together in the summers, in this small place. I despised Ian for not being at Eton, and he despised me for being there. But we played competitively together, and later we exchanged lies about our sexual experiences. He was always better than me at everything that needs skills and energy, but I've never needed to feel inferior about my love life.

My father always managed to take his leave in August. We would meet at Paddington and dine together at Simpsons', the constraints of a year apart thawing over the roast beef. Such as our intimacy ever was, we recovered it in the sleeping compartment, packing away our suits and ties and emerging onto the morning platform in clothes still stained with the previous year's sea. We always stayed in the Peter Aragons' farm, where the Gersons live now, and when my father came to the island for good, he bought the Aragons' own cottage, which was a two-roomed bothy then, built out of massive boulders, with stone weights holding down the turf roof. John Wesley slept in it on his only visit to Forway, when he found the natives unredeemed and unseemly. But by the time my father had begun on that conversion, I was seldom there. I sought quite different pleasures once I was an undergraduate, and even now, at the age when some men return to the pleasures of nature and silence, I felt more resigned to the island than devoted to it. I doubted whether I would return when my father was not there.

Parts of The Road on Forway are tarmacadamed, but it consists mostly of stone and shale. It winds along a little above the level of the cliff top, separated from a fearsome drop by an edging of rough ground. Occasionally it bends behind a small hill, but for most of its four miles there is a view of the endless sea, until it drops precipitously down into The Town. I drove cautiously. There are very few motor vehicles on Forway, but each is driven as though there were no others.

"So you don't think that U.D.I. will work," Tamara said.

"Of course it won't work. The whole idea is daft."

She seemed almost disappointed, and I went on, "How could it be on? I mean, even if the government left them to stew in their own juice, it's just impossible."

"Of course, nobody outside Forway knows about this yet," Tamara said.

"If they do, they will take it no more seriously than movements for Welsh or Cornish independence. Jokes one and all. But even if it came off, human nature would prevent it lasting." I felt, then, worldly, world-weary, infinitely more sophisticated than my elders.

"How do you see the scenario?" Tamara asked, as though she valued my opinion.

I took my fingers from the wheel to enumerate possibilities. "Most likely the government sends the troops in. That's what they would do in Shetland, say, or the Isle of Wight."

"They are more valuable than Forway."

"I know. This is a useless lump of rock without a deepwater harbour. All the same, they won't allow rebellion. Or another Power might decide not to wait for the judgement at The Hague and grab."

"And if they all wait and see?"

"I can tell you one thing that won't happen," I said with certainty. "This won't be an innocent island paradise uncorrupted by the twentieth century. That's pie in the sky. The first time there's trouble, an oil-slick, say, or a hurricane, or an epidemic, they will all run back to the nanny-state so fast, you won't see them move. That's the older generation. And the kids won't stand it for long. Not with all the airwaves bleeping out consumerism on every channel. You don't think the next generation will choose the simple life, do you? Not with all Pedro Barnes's money waiting to be spent out there in the big wide world."

"Will they get the money?" Tamara said.

"You heard Freya. She's handing the lot over to the islanders. Otherwise I suppose it would go to her own family. Pedro made a massive fortune, you know that, Tamara.

There are plenty of people on this island who have had a lifetime of simplicity and would choose Marbella or San Francisco any day. They know what they have been missing. I hear that Peter Aragon and his family are living in bliss near Torremolinos. And compared with the way they used to live, the Gersons' simple-lifery is just a sham. The people like Thetis Lisle or my father are a minority, doing their stints in the outside world and then coming here as fast as the ferry will bring them."

On The Road on Forway you can sometimes see no farther than the sea at your side and the bend a few feet ahead; and then, at other moments you can see its other end, three miles away across the hill. So I knew that some way ahead was Rik Gerson's old post-office van. It is the sort of road you have to attend to, but while we chatted I had registered that Tamara was something really special. Three hours since I first saw her, it had taken me to recognize the obvious. I admired her small, haughty nose. Her skin was in clear, almost primary colours, dead-white on her forehead and at the side where hair had kept the sun from tanning it, and strawberry-red on her cheeks. If she was wearing lipstick, it was skilfully disguised. The translucence of her mouth looked natural. And her eyes: poets have stolen all the analogies. I toyed with words, as I absent-mindedly turned the steering-wheel and changed the gears up and down. Sapphires? Aquamarines. Lapis lazuli? Hyacinths? No, they were a sharper, brighter colour than any of those. More like delphiniums at midsummer, or laundry-blue, a clear colour with no mauve in it, and, on the left iris, a fleck of yellow close to the pupil. She noticed me looking at her and said sharply, "Look out!"

I had not been concentrating on driving. I admit that. But I could have wrenched the wheel round, I could have braked to avoid the on-coming yellow van, if there had not been a sudden snap of something under the bonnet of Freya's van, and though my foot was off the accelerator pedal, the accelerator remained engaged. The throttle spring had broken. The brake did not seem to be working. It is strange how quickly the human mind works. In what felt like a split second I diagnosed the failure, I moved the gear lever to neutral, I pumped my left foot up and down on the unresponsive brake, I tried to hook my shoe under the accelerator to force it up—and the car skidded off The Road and down across the humpy, bumpy terrain towards the two-hundred-foot drop.

You will have read numerous descriptions, usually by definition invented, of cars and their passengers falling to their ends over a cliff. You will have seen even more mock-ups of the same event on the screen, stunt men leaping, dinky cars rolling, explosions of flame, gusts of black smoke. To a television generation it is almost boringly familiar. I prefer to leave the dramatic adjectives to your imagination.

I have to admit that I was not cool in the face of danger. I was in a useless panic and aware of impending death. Tamara Hoyland is made of better stuff. She dragged the sliding door on her side of the car back, looked out, quite cool, to see the ground outside. She said to me in a clear, commanding voice, "Magnus: open your door and jump."

I did. She did. I did not see her land, though it was later clear from her lack of injuries that she had done so like a gymnast. I fell awkwardly onto my shoulder. I heard the car scrape, fall, and splash into the sea. But the next thing I was conscious of was being in a strange bed.

❉

UNDAMAGED AND UNDETERRED, the redoubtable Tamara clambered down the cliffs with John Yetts and two boys who were camping out on The Hill in order to gain points for the Duke of Edinburgh's Award. Freya's van was beyond redemption and must be left to pollute the sea. Even if there were lifting gear on the island, it could never be driven again. But John Yetts felt personally responsible, he said, since if Freya had been driving, she would not have been agile enough to jump out. From the cliff top they could see the wreck, still recognizably a Bedford van, lying on its side like a discarded toy. The deep water of high tide had softened its fall, and it had neither burst into flames nor fragments.

"Only in my place yesterday," John Yetts said more than once. "And there was me showing it to Rik Gerson and telling him it would be better than his banger."

The climb down had to be made at low tide, several hundred yards along the cliff from the actual place where the van had fallen. Not even gulls-nesters or samphire-gatherers, legendary practitioners of now-obsolete trades, had ever managed to descend there. John Yetts watched approvingly as Tamara climbed down like a professional, leaving the boys gawping. Then they all made their way along the slippery shingle to the wreck.

It was the throttle spring that had broken.

"There you are," John Yetts said. "Snapped right off. Could happen anywhere." He unscrewed wheel nuts busily, determined to salvage at least the tyres before the tide turned. "Course, if there were a policeman on the island we'd have to get him to it," he told one of the soldiers and handed him a wheel to carry.

"Isn't there usually a policeman?" Tamara asked.

"Sergeant Hicks. He went sick, ten days back. Some sort of stomach trouble. Don't know when they'll get round to replacing him. Not much crime here after all."

Tamara put the coiled metal in her pocket and bent to give a hand with the dismantling. "Does anyone else ever drive this van? Except Mrs. Barnes, I mean?"

"Not that I know of. I know Sir Selwyn doesn't. He says there's no need to, place this size. But I've heard it's because his sight's bad." Tamara nosed inquisitively about the machine; her secret education had included some motor engineering. The brake pipes to two wheels were pinched together like hairpins. If they had been like that before the van fell, no fluid could have flowed through. "Better hurry, hadn't we?" one of the boys said nervously. The water was almost lapping round the van, and they would have to wade back to the cliff path. John Yetts filled his knapsack with anything he could salvage. "Worries you, does it, lad?" he said. "Don't suppose you're used to sea and cliffs where you come from."

"I come from Reading. And I don't care how soon I get back there. I feel like a prisoner here." Half-way up the cliff he dropped the wheel he was carrying, but John Yetts did not complain.

I WAS THE ONE WHO COMPLAINED, having been healthy all my life and consequently never before understood how unpleasant illness is. I only had a couple of bruised ribs and a minor concussion and was revoltingly sorry for myself. Dr. Thetis Lisle said I should stay on her ward overnight—no more than two rooms attached to the Lisles' house. At the time I was muddle-headed enough not to compare my own weakness with Tamara Hoyland's strength. In fact the contrast did not occur to me until the next morning when my father appeared and bawled me out in his best "accustomed to command" manner for showing myself up as a weak and feeble man, while Tamara had the heart and stomach of a king. He, like Godfrey Lisle, as I soon found, had been thumbing through the quotation dictionary for stirring words. Those were from Elizabeth I. When he turned up I was reading through the island Log; Godfrey Lisle had rushed in to press it upon me—he was always about twenty minutes late for everything—and rushed out again, telling me that he had always meant somebody to write a book about the island, and it was more my line than his.

My speciality, in fact, was writing racy but scholarly accounts of the adventures of famous explorers, the kind of book they might have written themselves if they were not too modest or too busy and could view their exploits with

posterity's eye. My greatest success had been with Fro-
bisher; at present I was overdue with Younghusband in
Tibet. I would not presume to say I had a writer's block,
but was beginning to believe that I just wasn't up to
Younghusband, not clever enough, not sufficiently imagina-
tive. I knew there was no future in self-castigation; the only
way to get a book written is to apply arse to chair and
write. But Godfrey Lisle's document was a welcome distrac-
tion from that thought.

It was a massive leather volume, bound with tarnished
brass, began by Godfrey Lisle's grandfather, that Glas-
wegian with a mission who had settled in Forway. He wrote
the regular, copperplate script of the conforming Victorian
and interspersed his words with prayers to and explanations
of the Almighty. He clearly thought of Forway as his sacred
charge, an attitude still apparent in his grandson, but his
original motives in settling in Forway in 1887 were perfectly worldly; he liked to be monarch of all he surveyed. He
was not welcomed then by the islanders, who at first
thought him an interfering busybody. The habit of taking
his advice and his gifts grew, however, and within not many
years had become the habit of jumping when he said jump.
By the time he was old he was round the bend, as far as I
could tell from his journal entries. He would have had to be,
to have perpetrated Trinder's Castle. I could well understand why Godfrey's father had been glad to hand the place
over to his cousin by marriage, Nonie Anholt's father.

Godfrey's own father was much more down to earth.
He evidently accepted his duty to Forway, partly, it
seemed, in pious memory of his mother, whose motives for
leading the uncomfortable life of a reformer were much
more altruistic than the old man's had been. But this second
Lisle regarded the place more as a job than a vocation. He
only wrote in the journal when something memorable hap-

pened, and he left out the prayers. There were not very many entries. Once starvation was banished, the population had risen dramatically, but its rise levelled out and then lessened; Godfrey's own entry for the current year showed that there were only twenty-nine children on the school roll.

Deaths, births, drought, and drowning; that was what the record consisted of, and only a sociologist would have wanted to make a book about it. Nothing in those pages explained to an outsider why those who passed their uneventful years on Forway should feel so passionately about preserving its life-style. Their only argument was that they were an endangered species. But I doubted whether conservationists would be able to drum up sympathy for such species as the natterjack toad if they had voices to speak for themselves.

In purely legal, unemotional terms, there were several items interleaved in the journal that might make useful evidence: rejections by Whitehall of appeals for money or practical help; refusals to maintain the ferry service; denials of any obligation to ensure means of communication; a letter of the most perfunctory regret when the helicopter service, being proved uneconomic, was withdrawn. Another sheet of paper showed that the government in Dublin had subsidized the ferry from Cork for years, and though that was probably through absent-mindedness, it still existed. Here were some expressions of fraternal interest from town mayors in Brittany, and here one from the Falkland Islands. In an envelope I found the case papers of a treason trial part-heard *in camera* in 1944. It referred to a man who seemed to have been an obscure version of Lord Haw Haw, employed by the Germans to preach surrender throughout camps in Italy to their prisoners of war. This man had been born on Forway, educated in Ireland, and had lived with his relations at Trinder's Castle from the age of eighteen until war broke out when he was twenty. He left for Cork, his ship was torpedoed, and he was rescued and captured by the Germans, for whom, after a while, he worked. His defence was to be that he was not a British subject, but the case never reached the stage of judgement, for while the trial was going on he was shot dead, while allegedly trying to escape. The man must have been a cousin of Nonie Anholt. I had never heard of him before, but the story left a nasty taste in the mouth.

Godfrey Lisle had taken over as captain of Forway on his father's death in 1950. He gave himself away in every word of his terse entries—a well-meaning, hard-working, slightly ineffectual man who did his best with responsibilities he did not question. I had just reached the great gale of 1975 when I heard my father's voice trumpeting along the passage and into the room.

"There's that girl, bright as a button, not a scratch on her, and here you are lying around like a wet rag . . . I don't know why you . . ."

My father had been disgusted with me for much of my life, as I went through a school career of muffing catches, missing kicks, and even fainting on parade at a corps display. He thought it was the last straw when I became a schoolmaster—until I turned into something even more reprehensible, a writer.

Luckily for me, Thetis Lisle came in before he could get very far with the catalogue of my inadequacies. I heard her outside the room, telling him about clinical shock; and I heard him grumping about weakness. Eventually Thetis sent him off and came back into the room. She was still wearing the apron in which she must have cooked her family's dinner and had pastry under her finger-nails. She sat down on the bed, reflectively picking it out.

I liked Thetis. I remembered her as Thetis Foggo, the

daughter of The Hotel. She had known her life plan from the cradle: off to London to get qualified as both dentist and doctor, then back to take charge of the island's health until her own gave out. So far she was thriving on delivering babies and laying out corpses, and there wasn't an operation in the book that she would not tackle if the weather kept the rescue helicopter at bay.

"So what do you think of Forway's U.D.I.?" I asked her.

She thought for a while before answering. "I feel it has been forced upon us. It wasn't an easy thing to decide. But how else can we save Forway? No matter which of the three Powers wins at The Hague, all of them are sure to like the idea of the oil rig. Our arguments about the survival of a small but viable community don't seem to register when there is oil and money at stake."

"Is this community viable? It's too small. Any crisis and you need outside help."

"Freya's generosity with the fruits of Pedro Barnes's genius has made us able to choose where the outside help comes from. We can buy it in."

"Everything?"

"Well, take my own work, for example; it's very different from general practice on the mainland. Of course we don't have those dreadful epidemics now; leprosy was endemic here in the seventeenth century, and there was a fearful outbreak of smallpox in the eighteenth, started by infection from the clothes of an islander who died on the mainland—his belongings were sent home to his family. That was the worst. But then there was cholera in the eighteen forties—the usual story of small isolated communities. And a bad flu outbreak just before the First World War, and another just after. We still suffer from 'boat colds,' even now."

"Boat colds?"

"New infections visitors bring in. Every time a ship used to call, the whole island was sneezing two days later. But that's more of an inconvenience than a disaster, and I can manage most things, if it's a case of having to. General practitioners on the mainland would be astonished at what one can do without the high technology. Like the Chinese 'barefoot doctors,' I've done a course in osteopathy, and in homeopathic medicine, and if necessary, I choose where to send my patients. Dublin, Paris, London . . . money is power."

"Muscle is power," I replied. "Three hundred Forway men won't be able to fight a detachment of marines. Or a gunboat. Half of you are kids and the other half geriatrics."

"What can we do but try it, if the only alternative is evacuating the island?" she asked unanswerably.

I said, "I just wish I couldn't foresee so much trouble. There are too many outsiders who could have an interest in this."

THIS NARRATIVE is obviously not about my own experiences only. I have collected the material, to make the story worth telling, so that I know now, as I did not at the time, that Tamara had told Mr. Black that she suspected outside interest too; but then, he had already told her that she was to trace to their source the invisible strings pulling the puppets. She also told him something that I did not notice as soon as she did: that most of the people of what one might call "active age" of Forway did not really have much time to think about politics.

It is necessary to understand that life there was always hard. Even in an era when food could be imported and help asked, except in the most isolating weather, those who lived on the island had to be able to take care of themselves and their dependants, and taking care of people on Forway was extremely time-consuming.

The effect of this simple fact of island life was that while some of the islanders were indulging in theories and fantasies about future independence and past legend (since the days of universal education one often heard allusions to Atlantis, Lyonesse, and Hy Brazil on Forway), most islanders were too busy scraping their livings from land and sea to think much about anything else. Far more important than the threats or plans for next year was the weather forecast for the next day: could one go fishing, plant seeds, repair the roof? Had enough turf been cut? Would it rain to refill the water butt? "It will keep the old ones happy," I heard one of the Yetts women remark about independence. And Jeannie Windows said it would keep them out of mischief. Mischief was something for which only the very young and the very old had time.

Perhaps it is natural, then, that few people in central London took the reports of the planned U.D.I. seriously either. I have been able to find out a certain amount of what went on inside government circles that May, for the old school network, deplorable but useful, gives me access to some sources of information.

On one side of St. James's Park, a suggestion that The Visit should be postponed was made only to brush aside, and at the other, Mr. Black's warning was treated with equal derision. So I hear, at least from my informant—whose identity I will not disclose. But I'm happy to say that Sylvester Crawford told me what went on at an editorial meeting of his current paper, his first since returning from El Salvador. I had mentioned U.D.I. to Thea on the telephone. Nobody had warned me it was a secret. Sylvester had offered the titbit about Forway to his editor, but the story was treated as a foretaste of the impending silly season. The conversation initially centred on dolly republics, Lilliput, and The Mouse That Roared. Flags of convenience, red-light islands, unlimited gambling, and tax havens were also mentioned.

The editor was as solemn and highbrow as his paper. He faced this problem, like everything else he encountered in life's obstacle race, seeing pitfalls and minefields ahead.

"It isn't as though they have done anything illegal," he said.

"Yet," said the Foreign Editor.

"It's a nice legal point anyway," contributed the legal affairs correspondent.

"Incitement to disaffection?"

The Foreign Editor drew a picture of a pimple in an expanse of sea and topped it with a Union Jack. "I don't think we need pay too much attention. It was probably all dreamed up by their tourist board. Have they got a tourist board?"

"Devolution is in the air."

The editor decided to send for the defence correspondent, who was in the Athenaeum discussing the defence tactics of the Carthaginians in the first Punic War with an Air Vice Marshall. When he arrived, he demanded maps and charts and his mini-computer and blinded everyone with expertise. The Foreign Editor expanded his doodle, to show a crowd of vultures waiting for the carcass of a dying animal.

"The trouble with independence," said Legal Affairs, "is that they would be too rich."

"How do you make that out?" asked the editor.

"I wish we had their problems," said the Foreign Editor and started drawing pound notes on his doodle.

"Territorial waters, tax haven, fishing rights—and oil. I imagine that's what all this is really about."

"So that's how the milk got into the coconut."

"Who would have thought that a miserable rock in the Atlantic would be so attractive," said Home Affairs.

"My dear girl, why do you think our ancestors went round painting them red?"

The editor naturally took for granted that anyone who wrote for the *Watchman* would not even consider the use of force. He said, "How could they be stopped, anyway?"

"Starve them out?"

"Run a blockade?"

"Sanctions?" said the editor in the tone of one using a dirty word.

"I didn't necessarily mean food," Home Affairs said huffily. "They will need other things."

"And they will have plenty of willing suppliers," said Foreign Affairs. "I dare say a cargo of gift-wrapped caviar is on its way already."

"And Hershey Bars."

"And ships bearing gifts from France, and from Ireland too. Damn it all," Legal Affairs protested, "we don't really know whom they belong to anyway."

"We could refuse them the facilities of the Health Service."

"There's an even better one in France. Didn't France once claim the island?"

"Stop their Social Security benefits."

"Refuse them landing rights at our ports and airports."

"Cancel their passports."

"You're making me feel quite sorry for them," said Legal Affairs.

"Well," said the editor, "I know what the government will do. Sweet F.A. I'll lay you anything you like that the Prime Minister is telling the Cabinet that they must be treated like naughty children."

"Spanked?"

"Shut up in a dark cupboard?"

"Deprived of sweeties?"

"You must have a fine collection of delinquent kids, I must say. No, they'll do what I always do with a naughty child."

Several of those present recalled with horror the hacks on the shin and the insults they had suffered from the editor's numerous children.

"The P.M.," said the editor, "will simply take no notice at all."

But as Foreign Affairs muttered to Sylvester as they left the meeting, "If we don't and the Russians do, the Americans will."

So Mr. Black, and his nameless colleagues, were the only officials to take the rumour seriously. He had his own plans, both of which he had made before ever his masters heard of the problem.

I have seen Mr. Black (in the distance, at a canteen table) since those days on Forway, and I can imagine his enigmatic smile as he read the proofs of an article to appear in that week's issue of the *Watchman*. Of that we heard nothing in Forway until later in the week.

THETIS LISLE INVITED ME TO DINNER THAT NIGHT. I believe she wanted to protect me from my father, but she said that her son, Humphrey, was longing to talk to me about writing. "He doesn't often get a chance to meet a real writer. Only the people who come for a trip here and then write something to set it against their income tax."

"I don't know that I count as a real writer."

"Nonsense, Magnus, you won the Peacock Prize."

So when the time came for me to rise from my bed of pain, I simply walked through the door. Another patient had come by then, Thetty Yetts, who intended to start a new tradition in Christian names. Whatever its sex, her baby would be called Independence.

Godfrey's grandfather had lived in the Lisles' house until his wife's death freed him to begin on The Castle. The formidable Jean Lisle, Godfrey's grandmother, had left uneradicated traces in the house, and Godfrey and Thetis seemed very snug amid their Victoriana. They had even left the pelmet hanging from the mantelpiece, and the browning photographs in tarnished frames upon it. Apart from their surroundings, however, the Lisles were a thoroughly modern family. The clothes worn by Humphrey and Kirstie could have come—probably did come—straight from the trendy shops of London. Thetis fed us on Greek-style shepherd's pie, made with aubergines and rather a lot of garlic, and we drank rough red wine.

I asked where the exotic vegetables came from.

"Israel, via Covent Garden."

"Will you still get them after U.D.I.?"

"I don't mind using local potatoes instead," Thetis said equably.

"We may make some separate trade agreements," Godfrey suggested. "None of these problems are insoluble."

"What will you do after independence, Humphrey? Are you going to be a doctor or a lawyer, too?"

"I had been planning to go into the Royal Navy, actually. I thought of training to be a marine designer. But in the circumstances . . ."

"That's not the only place to do the training," Godfrey said. "Nice though Greenwich is."

"Yes, but I'll have to do something that will be useful here, won't I? Like you and Mum, I mean. Forway's going to need it."

He did not look as though he intended sarcasm. I said, "You feel your place will be here, Humphrey?" He shrugged his shoulders, and Thetis said, "Don't imagine that we have brainwashed him, Magnus. It's all his own idea."

For that matter, nobody had brainwashed Thetis either. She had planned out her life at a very early age. I remembered her well at sixteen, four years older than myself. Elsewhere one might have derided her bossiness and called her "the head-girl type," and she might even have been a leader of girl guides and hockey captain. On Forway qualities that seem a little ludicrous to the hypersophisticated were valuable, and Thetis was admired then as now for her resourcefulness. I wondered whether Humphrey and Kirstie knew that their mother had once saved my life.

Annie Foggo was too grown-up by then to want to

come out fishing any more. She and Thetis were twins, but Annie had decided to leave school and would not have looked out of place on the Kings Road. Thetis still looked like a schoolgirl, unsophisticated in worldly things but wise in coping with natural ones. I rather fancied Annie, since I was precocious, but it was Thetis who kept us company in the boat. She and my mother were friends.

I was twelve, she was sixteen, and when the boom of the capsizing boat knocked me unconscious, it was she who held my face out of the water and propelled my inert body to the shore. During the following weeks it was she who nursed my inert mind, using, from common sense, the methods of psychiatric care that she was later to learn in her medical training. I went back to school at the beginning of the next term without being haunted by nightmares. The headmaster had expected a nervous wreck, which would have been a disaster in "common entrance year," but he got the same boy who had cheerfully left in July for the summer holidays with his mother; and I got a scholarship to Eton, too.

Godfrey was lucky to have Thetis, though neither he nor she would think of their lives together in those terms, for it had always seemed and been inevitable that they should marry and take over Forway. It looked as though Humphrey was accepting the same responsibility. The Lisles accepted their lifelong duties gracefully. I envied them all.

After dinner we sat by the fire of spitting driftwood, and Godfrey made notes for the speech he would have to make as Island Captain.

"Will you wear your chain, Dad?" Humphrey asked.

"And your red velvet gown?" said Kirstie.

Thetis raised her eyes from her tapestry. "Do, Godfrey, you'll slay them."

"I don't need all that stuff. They know who I am without it."

"Look." Thetis passed me two of the photographs from the mantelpiece, one of Godfrey himself, and one of his grandfather, each wearing a swathe of velvet and ermine, with a linked chain and medallion around his neck.

"I like this one best." Humphrey reached down another picture, of Grandfather Lisle in his regalia surrounded by seven other men wearing similar, if inferior, robes. "Grandfather brought all that stuff from London."

"It seems incongruous on Forway," I said.

"We are too dour here," Godfrey agreed. "That's what my grandfather told Granny Jeannie when he brought her here from the Clyde. 'A dour people,' he warned her. But she said they were no different from people all over. They needed soup in their bellies and tracts in their hands. She was always handing out tracts to seamen."

"And she wore stays all her life," Thetis added, stretching her own trousered legs luxuriously. "Can you imagine, stays and crinolines in our winds? She never left them off."

Kirstie Lisle was lying on the hearthrug colouring in a mathematical doodle. "Do you think we'll have a dance for independence, Mummy? You could wear a crinoline."

"Can you see your father on a dance floor?"

"I don't know," Godfrey protested. "I might perform the odd gyration in that cause." He was a mild-looking man with gentle eyes and a soft beard. Not dynamic, but reliable, and at ease with his life. He was surrounded by now with quotation dictionaries. "Do you think I should quote Queen Elizabeth at Tilbury?"

"What's wrong with Abraham Lincoln at Gettysburg?" Thetis said seriously. She had never been frivolous; even as a child, her work was directed and her words well spent.

"Or the American Declaration of Independence, that's

a good model," Humphrey said. He began to declaim. "We hold these things to be self-evident, that all men are created equal."

"I have been looking through the reference books," Godfrey said. "Cicero. Demosthenes. Winston Churchill. I feel there ought to be grand phrases for the occasion."

"The trouble is that all the modern equivalents have been debased," I said.

"I know. I don't want to stand up in The Square and talk about things like the Devolution of Power, or Self-Determination, or even Independence, really. All the words have so many overtones."

"Or undertones."

"I thought perhaps I could find some language that modern commentators hadn't used already," Godfrey said anxiously. "Something stately."

"Darling, you are silly," Thetis said. "You can't make stately speeches. That's not what Forway needs. You'll probably say something like 'That's it then, folks. On our own now.'"

"And the church bells will chime," said Humphrey.

"And we'll say three cheers," offered Kirstie.

And I said sourly, "And the parachuters will float down from the sky."

"I shall almost expect the skies to fall after that," Godfrey said in a sombre voice. "Don't imagine we've reached this decision lightly, Magnus. I once swore allegiance to the sovereign we are deserting."

"But in those days you believed that the sovereign would protect you in return," Thetis reminded him. I have often noticed that women are less influenced than men by such considerations as oaths and formal loyalties.

"Never mind, Daddy, perhaps they'll make you a sovereign instead. Then I can be a princess."

A peaceful family scene—interrupted, at that moment, by a distant noise, a low, reverberating rumble.

"Is that thunder?" Thetis said.

But Godfrey was already on his feet, shrugging himself into his anorak and doing up his shoe-laces. "Come on, Humphrey," he said. Humphrey was already at the door. I followed them.

"Not you, Magnus, you aren't well," Thetis called, but I went out into the windy night with the men and stood watching them as they quartered the sky with nose, ear, and eye, like hounds. Other people were coming out onto The Square too, more puzzled than alarmed.

"It didn't sound like a ship," one of the Windows men said. "Still and all, might just be worth—"

Some of the other men were on their way to the life-boat slip, when Godfrey called, "It isn't a shipwreck. Look."

In the distance, towards the Trinder's end of the island, the sky was smoky and inflamed against the scudding clouds.

"That's never The Castle on fire."

John Windows had brought out a tractor, and we climbed onto the trailer, some men clinging to the tractor itself, and chugged off from The Town.

It was not The Castle; it was only the Coastguard Station, disused since the early eighties—"all services must take their share of cuts in the economy"; there had been talk of turning it into a centre for birdwatchers.

The two young men who had been camping nearby were standing wringing their hands in incongruously tidy striped pyjamas. "We only had our billycans," one said. They were, it seemed, on an initiative testing trip.

The Coastguard Station was an inferno.

"That was quick," John Yetts said.

"Like when Pedro Barnes died," Godfrey muttered.

"Like a bloody inferno," John Windows said.

"Like an explosion," his brother Fred said. It was John Yetts who found the signature. It had been set on the ground far enough away not to catch a light, a largish plank of driftwood on which was written, in letters made uneven by protruding nails and gobs of oil, the words "Forway Liberation Front."

TAMARA HAD BEEN HAVING DINNER that evening with Selwyn Paull and Freya Barnes. She listened to their talk of independence, wondering about their motives. Selwyn said the timetable was all going according to plan so far.

Freya nodded. The arrangements with private hospitals were all completed; charter arrangements had been made for freight and passengers. An extremely complicated operation was being carried out, Tamara thought, like a well-organized military manoeuvre.

Selwyn mentioned two more schools with which retainers had been arranged, and he went through a list that he had written in a small leather notebook: cargo ships; suppliers of all soft and hard ware; services and the prices at which they would be available.

"All contingencies provided for," Freya commented. "Are you impressed, Tamara?"

"If they really are, yes. But what about emergencies?"

"Nothing we can't manage. It's not as though we have ever been very dependent on outside help here. Pedro was always convinced this could work."

"I have seen independence through in too many other places not to know the form," Selwyn said. "This is just another little blob on the map. No different from the Solomon

Islands, the New Hebrides, Belize, Antigua . . . easier really. We haven't any neighbours waiting to grab."

"*Quem deus vult perdere, prius dementat,*" Freya quoted. "Pedro always used to say that. 'Whom the gods wish to destroy, first they make mad.' The British government's treatment of Forway over the years has been quite mad. Years of neglect . . ."

"Save that for the press boys, my dear," Selwyn said.

"Are you planning a press conference?" Tamara asked.

"They will be here, you see, for The Visit. A better story than they ever hoped for. By the way, Freya, did I tell you, we have lined up that Aragon girl in New York; she's all set to deal with the U.N. It seems she's quite high up on the New York *Times* these days."

"Pedro always said she would go far. But what about other governments? We have always agreed that the announcement has to be everywhere simultaneously. The thing is, Tamara," Freya explained, "the British government won't care or dare to use force on us peaceful islanders if the eyes of the world are upon us. So we have to get everyone watching before they have time to pre-empt us."

"You talk about it so freely though," Tamara said. "Is this all meant to be a secret from London?"

"I doubt if anyone has heard anything, but they wouldn't take it seriously if they have," Selwyn told her. "They will think it's more of the same nationalistic talk. They have never taken much notice in Wales, after all, or Scotland, or even Northern Ireland. But nobody mentions it. Those journalists who were here yesterday, Hawker and his friend, they left empty-handed. I know, because he was up here pumping me, full of questions about my past, and my experience, and where I had served, and what I'm up to now, but he hadn't an inkling. And I didn't give anything away, I can tell you, I'm too downy an old bird for that."

"What was he asking you?"

"Oh, you know the kind of thing. A bit about the Council of Forway, a bit about foreign ships putting in, a bit about my own life—had I ever met Blunt and Philby at Cambridge . . ."

Back in London, Tamara had asked Mr. Black what crime the Forway men could be accused of so long as their independence was only in words and on paper. "They aren't likely to raise an army or anything," she had said. But he had reminded her of sedition, and harbouring the queen's enemies, and conspiring to breach the peace. She tried to imagine Freya in the dock at the Old Bailey and failed. It was all like a game, she thought.

But the noise that shattered the peaceful night was unlike any game. Tamara was under the table before her thoughts had caught up with her body. For a moment she was back in London, and Mike and Rory were dying all over again.

Freya was still sitting in her high-backed chair, though she trembled and was pale. Tamara emerged from her cover, ashamed to have protected herself before the old people. Selwyn had opened the door, and he and Tamara went out into the wind together.

"I thought your independence movement was non-violent?" she said.

"And so it is," he snapped. "This is nothing to do with us."

"A bit of private enterprise. But with what end?"

I ARRIVED BACK AT MY FATHER'S HOUSE in order to catch the first of the telephone calls. I did not know what the callers' drift was until the third. Then I ripped the cord from the wall. Some people had had an advance sight of what the *Watchman* was to publish the next day. Only too soon it would be all over the air waves.

Carl Hawker, the spy catcher, the mole hunter. The liar.

Those who had met him on Forway may not have known what he was famous for. They soon would. He could reel off names of men whose juvenile allegiances or adult treachery he had uncovered and displayed, as though they were his battle honours.

Carl Hawker—the damages payer—too late to save his victim's reputation. Hawker was no Chapman Pincher. He may have intended to follow in Pincher's footsteps, but they were creatures of different species. Hawker must have been sued for defamation more often than most journalists, and the reasons I had heard given for his keeping his job were too scurrilous to quote. But he is a pretty young man.

Carl Hawker's revelations tended to follow a well-mapped course. He would Name Names. Rival organs of the communications media would repeat what he had said, taking care to include quotation marks for self-protection. His victim would go into hiding, brazen it out with denials, or, less often, admit, apologize, and be destroyed. Members of Parliament would ask questions in The House. His victim's friends would write dignified complaints about witch-hunts to the posh papers. One of Hawker's stooges would rush into print with an eighty-thousand-word book. The victim's name would, in most cases, be rapidly forgotten, but his life would be ruined—or his family's lives: Hawker's victims were often safely dead.

That was Carl Hawker's circus. That's show business.

I had been able to regard Hawker's activities with light and cynical amusement, superior to human gullibility, until this moment. When the victim was my father, it seemed less funny.

For it seemed that in the next edition of the *Watchman*, Hawker would publish the suggestion that Selwyn Paull, K.B.E., was under suspicion of having been a member of that Cambridge circle of traitors so many of whose members Hawker had exposed, making Pincher's half-dozen into double figures; less reliably, of course.

Cambridge-educated, Cambridge-corrupted, one followed from the other. Guilt by association. My father had been at Trinity College, Cambridge. That much was true. He had never been in the Secret Services, nor in the Foreign Office, and Hawker did not suggest it. Instead, he listed the harm that could have been done to British interests overseas by a disloyal member of its colonial service. He described how someone in Selwyn Paull's position could have spent his career creating conditions in which the baneful influence of China or Russia would be welcomed by the natives from whom British protection had been withdrawn. The history of Third World politics in the last twenty years made it seem only too plausible. What secrets a man in that position would have been privy to; how useful to our enemies the alienating of those who had been our friends.

I gathered that the piece then asked where this man was now, and having located him on Forway, pinpointed that obscure island's position on world-shipping routes, in the world oil network, in the general defences of the western world.

❂

Freya had heard some gossip in The Town. "Do you know what they are saying?" she asked Selwyn Paull.

He said he had no time to listen to idle chit-chat. "You have no idea how many details there are to finalize."

Tamara had returned to the house to pick up her camera. She waited behind the kitchen door, listening, and loathing herself for doing so. Briefly she wondered whether any civilization was worth defending by uncivilized actions.

"That reporter, Selwyn. Hawkins. Harker. Hawker. You know who I mean."

"Foolish fellow. He went off empty-handed, I'm glad to say."

"It's the things he was saying about you, Selwyn. They aren't true, are they?"

"Wait a moment, my dear, let me just finish this list. Now then, what isn't true? What are you talking about?"

Freya's voice was weak, quavering. Tamara felt sharply indignant that her tranquillity should have been disturbed, ill-founded though it may have been. "Selwyn, they say that Mr. Hawker told them you had been . . . that you had . . . I don't know how to say it . . ."

"Come on, woman, come along."

"That you were a traitor. While you were in the colonial service. That you had been in the pay of the enemy."

"What enemy? I was a marine during the war."

"Not the Germans. Like Burgess and Maclean . . . the Russians." Her voice was very low, as though she could hardly bring herself to express the accusation, but Selwyn Paull's reply was at full pitch.

"The Russians? In the pay of the Russians? What are you talking about?"

"It's what they are saying. That you were working for them all the time you were—"

Selwyn Paull believed in the good old-fashioned virtues of self-control, obedience, and discipline. But temper, normally suppressed by will power, was natural to him, and now he gave way to it, so that Tamara wondered whether he would, literally, have an apoplectic fit. She could see Freya's speckled hand trembling on the arm of the chair. When her voice could be heard through his, she was saying, "I shouldn't want to carry on if I thought . . . well, I mean, our independence wasn't going to be . . . it wasn't going to do any harm to England."

"Freya—"

"It all seemed such a wonderful idea. You persuaded me. You convinced me. But I don't want to give the Russians a foothold in the Atlantic. Perhaps I have been wrong all along."

"Freya." Selwyn drew a chair close to hers and sat down, taking her hand, summoning all his powers of soothing persuasion. "All these years we have been friends, Pedro and you and I. So much we have come through together. All we have experienced together. Are you really going to believe a malicious rumour spread by a tuppenny ha'penny scandalmonger from a Fleet Street rag? Haven't I deserved something more than that?"

He may never have been in the diplomatic service, but he had winning ways. Tamara found herself able to under-

stand how he had persuaded Freya and the other islanders
to be enthusiastic about his schemes; how he had converted
them, until Godfrey and Freya at least became more royal-
ist than the king. He managed to calm Freya down. The
fact is, as Tamara realized, she was the sort of woman who
was lost without a man to lead her, even though she seemed
to be, in Mr. Black's definition, the "front woman." A leader,
presumably Selwyn Paull; and a visionary, Godfrey Lisle;
Tamara had identified them all. She was concealed behind
the house as the leader and the front woman tottered towards the meeting of their congregation, and in her mind
she translated Mr. Black's list to the blind, the deaf, and the
lame.

THE ISLAND MEETING TOOK PLACE IN THE CHURCH. I'd been watching out for Tamara. When she slipped in at the back, Godfrey Lisle was on his feet. Godfrey always repeated himself and was hammering home his point that terrorism was in nobody's interest, when the assembly was transformed by Tamara's addition to it.

"It isn't any good to us, it isn't any good to anyone. It won't bring us independence, it will destroy our chance of it. It's unforgivable. It's monstrous." He looked disorganized, slightly scatty, unlike the Island Captain, velvet-robed or not, who planned to rival Winston Churchill or the first Elizabeth in his speech-making. "The very last thing we need now, the very last, is violence. It's the one way to make absolutely certain that we shall never get what we want. Whoever on this island has been trying to help our cause in this lunatic way—"

"Are you sure that the aim was to help our cause?" Thetis Lisle put in.

"What do you mean?"

"Maybe there is someone on the island who does not want us to save it."

"But we all agreed. Everyone on Forway—"

My father interrupted with the authority of experience, and my heart bled for the old man, although all his islanders turned to listen attentively to him. As two members of a family alone, we could be mutually irritated by each other, but I would have given anything to protect him from what I feared was to come. He said, "Let us consider this logically and calmly. Luckily there is no great harm done. Nobody was hurt. The property was abandoned and had no value."

"It was an ancient monument," Thetis Lisle said.

"There is that, of course." My father glanced apologetically towards the back of the room, where Tamara Hoyland was sitting.

"A piece of old Forway," one of the Windows women said sentimentally.

"There won't be much of old Forway left if we don't get our independence," Godfrey groaned.

"Look." My father held up his hand for silence again. "As it happens, Sergeant Hicks is away from the island."

"Bloody funny that is too, while you're about it," one of the Windows said. "Just like he'd been poisoned. Groaning and vomiting he was . . ."

"Anyway," my father persevered, "there is no proper authority to investigate at present. I don't think it matters. We can manage without that Coastguard Station."

"What we can't do without is the coastguards," John Yetts muttered.

"When we are independent, we can restore the coastguards," my father said impatiently. "I can understand that someone thought it was a good place to make a gesture. It's just that it was such a damn silly gesture. Somebody's been watching too much television. This isn't Ireland. The British government would like nothing better than an excuse to send in a peacekeeping force. It's only so long as we do nothing, absolutely nothing, that they could claim was breaking the law or endangering people or property that their hands are tied. We have to keep the situation so that they lose all international support if they try to suppress us. Blowing things up is just playing into their hands."

My father already looked as though something in his world had collapsed. So did Freya Barnes.

I marvelled that Forway's future could matter so much to these two old people. I remembered a dictum of George Orwell's, that it could not be altogether an accident that nationalists of the more extreme and romantic kind tend not to belong to the nation they idealize; like Napoleon, for example, a Corsican, or Hitler, an Austrian. The two major enthusiasts in this room were neither of them natives of Forway. My father had lived all over the world and been involved in affairs of state. And Freya? She too knew more of the world than just Forway. When Pedro Barnes was a professor at Oxford, she had been hostess to scientists and statesmen.

Perhaps this was my father's, and Freya's, final fling, their last chance to make a mark on the world. Yet it was the native islanders, the Yettses, Aragons, Windowses, Foggos, and Lisles, who were gambling their homes and capital and livelihood on a cause I thought lost before it had begun. Looking round their self-reliant faces, and remembering pictures of the islanders of St. Kilda when they had to evacuate their lonely home, I almost wished that Forway could win.

"Is the plan still a secret?" John Windows asked. "Has anyone been talking?"

"Not outside the island, surely," my father said. People were shaking their heads, looking round for betrayers. "All our contacts with suppliers have been in the name of the Forway Trust. There have been no mentions at all of political changes. And there's nothing on paper. The press releases are under lock and key. Aren't they, Rik?"

"Nobody has seen them," Rik Gerson said firmly. "I would know if they'd been disturbed."

I held up my hand, and my father, who seemed to have taken control of the meeting from the Island Captain, said, "Yes, Magnus?"

"I should have thought word of your U.D.I. plans could easily have got out. You aren't very cautious about discussing it. I only arrived here this week, and it was no secret from me."

"We are careful about outside ears. And there are few outsiders to hear this year. Haven't you noticed that there are no holiday-makers yet? We have refused bookings."

"Some of my regulars were ever so disappointed," Annie Foggo said.

"We were glad of the excuse to put people off," said Lena Gerson. "Holiday accommodation is far more trouble than I expected."

"There have been outsiders here, though. What about those two journalists who took my place on the *Eurydice?*"

"And the party from the *Eurydice* itself," Tamara murmured.

"They heard nothing. All that lot was interested in was spending their money. They wanted local crafts."

"I sold three knitted berets," Lena Gerson said. My father called everyone's attention. "That really is not the point," he said. "What we are assembled to discuss is last night's outrage. Now, I think I can safely promise that there will be no retribution or recriminations. What's done is done. But no doubt the perpetrator of the outrage will now realize how wrong he was."

"Who's to say he's here?" called one of the Foggo boys. "We're all here."

"What about that Irishman up at The Castle then? And

Mrs. Anholt isn't here either. She never comes to our meetings."

A mutter rose in the room. "That's right. The Irishman. Bombs, explosions. Terrorists."

"We don't know anything about him," Godfrey Lisle shouted above the growing noise. "Just because he's from Ireland—"

"We don't deserve independence if we start judging people by their accents," Thetis Lisle said in her ripe Forway voice. According to dialect specialists, the Forway accent was that of North-West England, fossilized for a century, but nobody knew why.

"Anyway, what possible motive could he have?" Godfrey shouted.

Such meetings always end inconclusively, and I did not think that the experience had been cathartic either. We left dissatisfied, eyeing each other suspiciously.

"And we were so united," Freya said sadly as she came out leaning on my father's arm.

"I suppose you expected Utopia," I said sourly.

"Why not?" she snapped back.

"Utopia has a better climate, for one thing."

"Other places have climates. We have weather," my father quoted.

How right he was. On Forway the hourly changes from rain to shine, from calm to gale, from warm to icy, were so much part of life as hardly to attract attention, and the fact that when we gathered in The Church an almost horizontal fine rain had been enshrouding the island, and that now it was brilliantly clear, with not a cloud to be seen, hardly deserved comment.

A helicopter was landing. "That will be the security men," my father said, and he and Godfrey went off to meet them. I almost stopped him. But then I thought that if the helicopter had brought an advance guard of press blood-hounds, Godfrey, with his massive and manifest simplicity, would be a better protector than myself.

Freya said that she was going to eat something with Annie Foggo at The Hotel and then go out in her boat. I asked Tamara to walk up The Hill with me and was sur-prised when she agreed. I did not know then that she wanted to pump me for information.

The Cork ferry had called at dawn, so we collected some newspapers and food and walked off together. I could feel indulgent glances following. We were made for each other, I thought they would be saying, a handsome couple, well matched.

Tamara had the knack of making people talk—or, per-haps, of making those who loved her talk. Ian had been massively indiscreet about his work, as I was later to hear. By the time she and I had reached the remains of the light-house, Tamara had extracted from me an account of every-thing I had done, seen, and heard since arriving on Forway. I was putting out my wares to attract her during those days, all those practised tricks that experience had taught me were attractive to attractive girls. I was despicable. I was like a dog rolling submissively onto its back, I was like a peacock spreading its tail. Tamara was putting out her wares too. Her alert and apparently sympathetic interest en-couraged me to tell her everything—and not only me. A good many people on Forway told her more than they real-ized. Like me, they probably did not recognize that she was interested in their information more than their personalities; nor had I recognized, as she did, that we were seeing the start of a classic destabilization exercise. If distrust and unease were created among those close-knit islanders, per-haps by the sabotage of main services, such as they were,

the island would ripen for authority's, or an enemy's, plucking. I merely thought that the islanders were edgy, and if I
considered the idea of a Forway Liberation Front at all, it
was only to dismiss it as a juvenile extravagance.

✸

MORE OFTEN THAN NOT, the top of The Hill was sheeted in cloud, but today Tamara Hoyland and I could see the whole of Forway and the unusually numerous ships in the sea around it. My bruised ribs were aching but I tried to suppress the thought, for Tamara looked so new-minted and glossy. On other women that brilliant sun would have revealed flaws. It highlighted her perfection.

She told me about her archaeological survey and the evidence of the past about us. "So much of the work has been done for me," she said sadly. "Ian saw pretty well everything when he was a schoolboy." She had his notebook in which he had written notes and drawn maps and accurate, if inartistic, sketches.

"I wonder why he never became an archaeologist himself," I said. As far as I knew then, Ian's chosen career had been that of an administrative civil servant.

"He wanted to influence the present, not just record the past," Tamara said. I did not then recognize the self-justification in her voice. Nor did I know that she was working even at that moment, while we sat on the damp turf and while I relished the sun on my face and the prospect of pleasure with my companion. I was an arrogant man, at least about women. I was not much afraid that Tamara

Hoyland would reject me. So far in my life, I had been more pursued than pursuing.

You cannot see land from Forway, nor is it visible from other lands. What a horrible shock it must have been to a sailor who unexpectedly saw that gaunt threat looming out of an empty sea and felt the waves and the tide drawing his ship ever closer to its hidden teeth. The lighthouse beside whose stump Tamara and I now lounged had been built by a public subscription in England and Ireland in the last decade of the nineteenth century. An American steamship had been wrecked on Forway in 1888, and a small plaque fixed to the lighthouse wall recorded both its name and the generous donations made by Americans to the cost of the lighthouse.

"I hate the sea," I said.

"After living here? I do too, but to Ian it was a native element. I don't mean he loved it, just that it was like the earth or the air, an inevitable part of life."

"He could cope with it. I get seasick. And I have never got over being afraid, which seems silly when I did spend my holidays fishing and sailing here."

"I'd have thought you would be too used to it."

"It's all right in a big boat like the *Eurydice*. But my mother was drowned in a small boat, and I've never trusted them since."

"Here?"

"Yes. Even people who have lived here all their lives get taken by surprise by the weather. That's what happened to her."

"Was she alone?"

"Thetis Foggo—Thetis Lisle—and I were with her. Her head was hit when we capsized. We were picked up quite quickly, but she was dead."

"I am sorry," Tamara said.

"At least half the tombstones here are for people who were drowned. The ones on the north side of The Church are those without names. 'Known unto God,' they put, if they buried them at all. Until Godfrey's old grandfather took charge, I doubt if they bothered with such niceties."

"Well, I can see why you are not fond of small boats."

"It would not count as much excuse here, actually. There is not much life for you on Forway if you can't rise above that kind of thing. I think a lot of people feel the only place they can get away from each other is at sea. And of course, one needs the fish. Even old Freya still goes out spinning for mackerel."

"I know. She's going today, I'm afraid."

Several small boats had put out after the meeting. One had to take advantage of the weather. This was not a place where there was any point in making plans before waking up to see if the elements would cooperate. Now I could see one of the Windows brothers hoeing his vegetables and the two Yetts pacing their ground together, coats, caps, and strides matching. Lena Gerson was tugging a thin cow towards her shed; every line of her body indicated curses. There was no movement to be seen at Trinder's Castle, though I could see the oldest Aragon man picking shellfish near the causeway ahead of the rising tide.

"It's all really very small," Tamara said.

"Five point nine six square miles. About four thousand acres or sixteen hundred hectares. Population two hundred and seventy-three."

"Didn't the Duke of Wellington say that a regiment should be no more than five hundred men because that was the largest number one commanding officer could know by name?"

"I imagine the figures for a self-governing nation are somewhat greater," I said acidly.

As though absent-mindedly, I put my arm around her shoulder. She fitted neatly into the curve. I hoped that in her, as in me, instinct would take over from thought. But she soon moved away from me and got up to start prodding at the ground and picking up small objects from it. I turned my attention to the papers I had brought up from The Town.

On Thursdays the papers came via Cork, so Forway men saw the *Irish Times* and the *Cork Examiner* as often as the *Times* and the *Guardian,* but the London papers that had reached southern Ireland by Wednesday afternoon usually came on the ferry too.

Carl Hawker's companion, Maggie, whose surname, apparently, was Macaulay, had got her pen to paper as quickly as he. One of the London papers carried an article by her about the *Eurydice's* cruise round the British Isles, and since it was written as though its author had been present throughout, I knew that much of the copy was derived from the brochure; indeed, I recognized some of the hyperbole. The illustration was a photograph of the passengers disembarking at Holyhead for a visit to Anglesey and the famous garden at Bodnant; Maggie Macaulay and Carl Hawker, presumably, had caught the train to London instead. Holyhead was the next port on the planned itinerary after Forway. The faces in the photograph were familiar to me: the lawyer from Boston, the famous writer, and the old woman in her fisherman's sweater, at last defeated by the exertions of the trip and being wheeled off the gangway. I knew that girl, at one side of the wheeled chair, while a sailor helped her on the other side. It was the girl I had seen in the Hebrides, dark-haired, dark eyes. It was not the young woman I had watched disembarking at Forway.

Were there two women companions? Two women who wore enveloping clothes and shared the tiny cabin?

I shrugged the minor perplexity away. I did not intend to write about the cruise of the *Eurydice* myself, so it was of no importance. I turned pages, marvelling as always that the hot news in England should be so different from that in Ireland. The *Irish Times* devoted its front page to the troubles in Northern Ireland which were not mentioned in the London *Times* that day at all. Another cardinal had been making appeals. Another American senator had arrived on a fact-finding mission. A terrorist had been recaptured after his escape from a Dublin gaol. His girl-friend was still on the run: Emma Hurst, otherwise known as Dierdre Tyrone. Two mug-shots were shown, full face and profile; and the girl was the one who had left the *Eurydice* at Forway with the game old woman.

In other circumstances I should certainly have doubted my memory. But the atmosphere of Forway just then was one of melodrama, and it seemed perfectly likely that a murderous terrorist should be on the island.

I lay back on the grass to think about it, some of my mind wandering to the closeness of Tamara Hoyland and to the skin-stinging brightness of the sun on my face.

Dierdre Tyrone: another English public-school girl bewitched into criminality by the legend of Holy Ireland. It was easy to see what she had done. Several of the *Eurydice*'s passengers had remarked on the perfunctory nature of the passport and customs formalities between British and Irish ports, for this shipful of passengers of all nationalities. A carefully synchronized operation would have been almost fool-proof.

The old lady would have come on board at Southampton with her innocent companion, who was seldom seen, and then only when well muffled up. Disembarking at Galway, they would have met Dierdre Tyrone, who escaped from prison and was anxious to enter the U.K. She would have returned to the ship in the guise of the companion who had been on board for days before the notorious terrorist was known to have got free. No doubt there would be some check on passengers at Southampton, especially as the *Eurydice* was calling in the Channel Islands on the way there. I had heard the women, foiled by a Saint's Day from buying Waterford glass in Waterford, promising loudly to "hit the stores" in Jersey, so presumably customs officers would be waiting to pounce. But Dierdre Tyrone could safely leave the ship at one of the British ports of call before that: Holyhead, or Scilly, or Falmouth, or Forway, and the original girl, who would have made her way there by other means, could replace her again.

But unless Dierdre Tyrone had returned to Ireland on the Cork ferry this very morning, and she would hardly wish to do that, she must still be on the island; it was not hard to guess where she would be.

TAMARA HAD HEARD OF DIERDRE TYRONE earlier in the day, over breakfast with Freya Barnes. Unfortunately, but naturally, she did not take Freya very seriously. Tamara had seen the girl herself, a gentle creature with a degree in archaeology, and liked her. Freya was seventy-five and for most of her life had seemed much younger than her years, so it was not surprising that bereavement should have aged her, especially since she carried around so much surplus weight and chain-smoked. Her physical health seemed good, and her face was still beautiful. But her behaviour worried Tamara, though she did not know how much she should worry. She had not known Freya well after her only previous visit to Forway, and for all she could tell, Freya had been wandering in her thought and speech processes for years. Perhaps it was her native characteristic to lose track of her anecdotes, forget proper names, and change the subject of conversations. Perhaps a gentle inconsequentiality had been part of her famous charm.

Nor did Tamara know what her responsibility was as nothing more than the girl-friend of Freya's dead son. She knew that there were no other relations, except for the unattractive Gersons, with whom she would be reluctant to discuss Freya. Tamara decided to have a word with Thetis Lisle and meanwhile stayed on in the cottage with Freya, chatting, picking up what she dropped, turning off the gas when she left it on, stubbing out the cigarettes she abandoned, and worrying gently about the old woman's future. Uncomfortable words tittuped in and out of her mind, like "senile dementia" and "irreversible deterioration" and "confused geriatrics," all the ghastly jargon of a society in which the natural incidents of life and death are regarded as pathological. For all that was wrong with Freya was old age —life itself, in fact, a condition for which there can be only one cure.

Luckily the episodes of "wandering" were not so frequent as to make life with Freya uncomfortable, and at breakfast that morning Freya had entertained her guest with all the sparkling concentration that had subjugated generations of her husband's students.

Time diminishes age difference. Freya was describing a conversation in which Tamara visualized two very old women talking about the distant past. Yet Nonie Anholt was not much more than sixty; and when she and Freya recalled meetings in Oxford, it was an Oxford in which Nonie was a young and frivolous visitor to a house where Freya presided as a matron. "I forget who brought her to the house first," Freya mused. "There were so many boys, each so self-centred, and all so hard to tell apart. So many young men who thought that they were the first people in the world to understand anything, so arrogant. I used to make them dried egg and carrot cakes. Some of them were sent parcels from the family estates and then they brought me cream and butter; against the law, of course. Nonie married one of them, one of the rich ones. I must admit he did look very dashing in his uniform. The Greenjackets. But I could see what he'd become, a real blimp. You can always tell."

"And did he?" Tamara had asked.

"He was killed in North Africa. But Nonie's boy is ex-

actly what his father would have been. A stockbroker, I believe. He came here to see her and was pathetically embarrassed. He worried what his neighbours would have said."

"I thought it was pretty ghastly at Trinder's Castle."

"Oh well, poor old thing, she can't cope." There was a
note of complacency in Freya's voice. "I go and see her
from time to time. Actually she was very pleased to see me
yesterday."

"Was anyone else there?"

"The Irishman, you mean? I didn't see him, though
Nonie had a new bruise on her cheek. It might have been
dirt though. Dirt . . . dirt . . ." Tamara had noticed several
times that Freya's mind seemed to get stuck; she would
repeat the same word or phrase like a scratched gramo-
phone record. Freya sat murmuring that monosyllable and
rubbing at her own cheek. There was ash on her hand, and
she left a smudge where she had seen one on Nonie Anholt.

Tamara took Freya's hand in her own reassuring grasp.
Tamara's hands were always warm. Freya stopped speaking
but puffed at her cigarette and drank more tea. She went on
in a stronger voice, "There was someone there, though."

"Who was that, Freya?"

"A girl. I've seen her somewhere. Seen her picture."

"A pale girl with light blue eyes and mousy hair?"

"That's the one."

The two old women had been sitting in that dusty ruin
of a library. "Not much like the rooms we used to meet in,"
Freya said. "I couldn't help remembering Pedro's work-
room in Boars Hill. Not that I believe in living in the past.
But the contrast . . . Anyway, she didn't see me. This girl, I
mean. I was sitting on that old Koole settee with my back to
the door, and of course it is higher than my head. Very uncomfortable when you are my size, I must say. The girl was

terribly cross when she saw me. Thought she'd been indiscreet."

"What had she said, Freya?"

"Nothing I could understand. Something about a boat that was overdue. I suppose they are on their way, they never stay very long. She was telling Nonie to go to bed and keep quiet. Like that poem, 'Watch the wall my darling and let the gentlemen go by.' Not that this was at all poetical, she sounded too fierce. And when she saw me sitting there, 'Who's this?' she said, as though I had no right in the place, and then she dragged poor Nonie out into the passage and I heard her asking all about me and saying she had told Nonie there were to be no visitors. Nonie kept saying that I live all alone and wouldn't tell anyone anything even if I knew what to tell, which I don't."

"And haven't you any idea what it was she wanted you not to tell?"

"It would be something to do with the Irish boy, of course. He's bewitched the girl, in the same way that he bewitched poor Nonie. Men like that . . . of course, Nonie's been sheltering these Irish criminals at The Castle for years. They hide out there till the heat's off them. It's all revenge. She's getting her own back."

"Does everyone know she shelters criminals?" Tamara could not help sounding surprised.

"I don't suppose so. There's no secret that she has Irish visitors at The Castle. There won't be many people who remember that old story of her cousin."

"Haven't you ever felt you should—well, tell somebody?"

"We believe in living and letting live on Forway. They don't do any harm."

"Who blew up the Coastguard Station?"

"Not them. Why should they care for Forway's independence?"

"Do you know who did, Freya?"

"Just a naughty boy. It was only a prank. Selwyn is making too much fuss altogether, in my view."

"Some prank."

"I'm just not sure who would have known how to do it. I don't suppose explosions are as easy to perpetrate as all that. Of course, Pedro would have known what to do . . ."

Freya sounded almost . . . what was it? Wistful? Envious? As though she would have liked to take some dramatic action herself? "I expect Ian could have managed it," she added.

"Probably," Tamara murmured drily; she was thinking that she could have managed it herself too and wondered whether she would ever have occasion to use that part of her versatile training.

Freya's eyes had fallen closed, and her breathing slowed, but she snored once loudly and woke herself up with the noise. She said, "I was thinking of Ian. I have to remind myself he's dead. I never have to do that with Pedro."

"Ian was away so much of the time, that's probably why."

"Yes. Away but alive. And now he's dead . . . but still not here. I want to give you his things, Tamara." She rose and went to her desk. "Here. His cuff-links and his emerald ring."

"I never saw that."

"It's a bit flamboyant to wear nowadays. It belonged to my grandfather. I should have liked you to have his watch, and the monogrammed pencil he always used, the one George V gave Pedro's father when they served on the

Bacchus together. But as you know, nothing survived the crash."

"I remember the pencil. Gold, with *B* on it. Was it *B* for *Bacchus?*"

"*B* for Barnes. Pedro's father performed some service for the king—prince, as he was at the time. I never heard what; it was probably something highly disreputable, or the monogram would have been a royal *G*, I expect. Here." Tamara took the sad little relics. The ring, a cameo-cut emerald, fitted on her third finger, and she put it on her left hand. Freya said, "You go ahead. Selwyn is calling for me so we can go to the meeting together. I thought I might go fishing afterwards. Mackerel for supper."

Tamara knew that Freya had always used her boat as an escape route and that she might be feeling in need of her favourite therapy today. But she could not help worrying at the thought of Freya alone in her small cruiser. Who had the right or the duty to prevent her going? Should she be kept out of danger? For if her mind wandered when she was far out at sea, goodness knows what could happen.

But then, Tamara thought brutally, even if Freya did kill herself, it might be better for her than dying slowly with diminishing faculties. Please God, she prayed, safe in praying because she knew she would not be heard, don't let me live to be old. She felt a horror for the frailty of human understanding. The physical decline was bearable, one could watch Freya lean on a stick, one could count her wrinkles with the dispassion that Tamara so far felt about her own incipient blemishes, but to notice a memory, a mind, a determination, being dissipated into oblivion . . . far be it from me, Tamara had thought early that morning, to stop Freya from doing something dangerous or even fatal.

FREYA'S BOAT WAS FATAL TO HER THAT DAY. Tamara and I watched from the lighthouse hill as one of the boys who always hang around the boats rowed her out to the small cabin cruiser. We saw her hand the boy something.

"Does she pay them?" Tamara asked.

"Sweets. Or probably some cigarettes," I told her, having earned them myself in my time.

Binoculars trained, we both saw her put a cigarette in her mouth. We watched her strike several matches.

"She'll have to go below to light it," I said idly.

"She must smoke forty a day," Tamara said.

Freya opened the low door and let herself down into the cabin, a small cramped space with hardly room for a fat woman beside the engine housing and the equipment of a primitive galley.

There was a smell of gas, young Humphrey Lisle said later, weeping. He had noticed it when he pulled the dinghy alongside. "I told her to look out," he cried. "I know the smell of bottled gas when I smell it. Freya couldn't smell things any more, we all know that." We all knew that. Old age and smoking had completely destroyed Freya Barnes's sense of smell.

Out of the wind, in the shelter of the cabin, she must have struck another match; and inside the cabin, hermetically sealed until she opened its door, gas must have been leaking to fill up the atmosphere. The little boat was called *The Pedro and Freya*. It exploded like a petrol bomb.

For some reason that I did not understand until much later—for I did not know the circumstances of his death then—Tamara, beside me, was saying, "Ian, Ian, Ian," over and over again.

This narrative would not make legal evidence. It is mostly hearsay; at first hand, of what Tamara eventually told me; at second hand, of what others had said to her; at third hand, of what those others had heard and passed on.

But our view of Freya's death was immediate. Although Tamara had been thinking of it with equanimity, she was not calm at the sight. And that, deplorable though such a reaction was at the time, was a relief to me. For I did not relish being inferior to a girl, even this girl, in all the manly virtues. Equality is easier to write propaganda for than to experience. Even a properly reconstructed male like myself found it hard to be weaker and less able to cope with emergencies than this smallish girl. Is that my excuse for the sour tone with which I speak of Tamara Hoyland's blatant superiority to Magnus Paull, of the superiority of the girl I adore to me? My excuse for the satisfaction with which I realized that I could face what she could not—that is, going down to The Town and helping to pick up the pieces?

Not that there were many pieces. A lot of people were trying to pick them up. It was simply a question of rescuing other property, dousing flames, and dunking cinders. Freya could not have survived that first blast for an instant. Most of us could do nothing but watch.

We agreed that it was obviously an accident; that Freya knew, as all boat owners know, the danger of leaks from the bottled-gas cylinders; that the disaster was a coincidence, unconnected with The Visit due the next day. My father said that nothing need change, nobody is indispensable, none of us is immortal. Others agreed that Freya would have wished things to carry on without her.

One hovered, helplessly.

After a while I went to offer to do something, for the second time. But the necessary work was better done without a townee landlubber.

Viewed in ignorance, the scene could have seemed as pretty as a boating lake in an amusement park, a pretty coloured picture with gaudy boats bright in the sun, and people moving about with the rapidity of a comically speeded-up film. But only a small shift in perception, and it became one of those all too familiar pictures of a disaster area, where human activity seems as frantic and hurried as that in a disturbed ants' nest. Only one other boat had caught completely on fire, and jets of water were dousing its flames. All the others had been moved away in time so that there was a bare cordon of empty water around the patch where oil was still burning, speckled with pieces of plastic and painted metal.

The older men were still working purposefully, but the resilient young already, or perhaps always, unaffected by tragedy, whizzed around in their boats as though emergency had loosened inhibitions. I watched one of the Aragon boys leaning out of the dinghy as his brother paddled through a channel of debris. He picked something out of the water, which he then pushed furtively under his sweater.

Godfrey Lisle was one of the last to come wearily up the steps, mopping his wet face. The horror of the event was compounded by a rare warmth in the air. It should have been a lovely day. Godfrey said what everyone had been saying.

"She must have known. We have all heard it so often. Check for gas leaks. Light a match and—whoomph," he said dismally.

Anona Aragon's shrill voice rose at the back of the crowd. "There Freddie, isn't that what I'm always telling you? What's that you've got there? Give it here. Freddie, give me that immediately. Where did you get . . . ?"

Freddie Aragon had been forced to surrender a watch to his mother.

"That's Pedro Barnes's chronometer. The gold one they gave him when he . . ." Thetis Lisle's voice faded away. Freddie Aragon hung his head and scuffled his feet, and his mother's attitude changed from anger to protectiveness. Nobody else but her should accuse her son.

My father's voice was still weak, but I think everyone heard it. "Looting. Terrorism, and now theft. What next? Anarchy?" For a moment he looked like my idea of a prophet in the Old Testament, his eyes raised to heaven, tragedy in his squared lips. Then he was the old administrator again. He said more loudly, "Our only hope is to abide by the law. We have to be able to guard ourselves from ourselves as well as from outside oppressors. Theft has been unknown on Forway."

Freddie Aragon was crying quite loudly. "I didn't mean it," he wailed.

"What are you talking about, theft?" Anona Aragon shouted. "My Freddie wouldn't steal anything. Who do you think you are, saying things like that? You're nothing but an incomer, when all's said and done. And worse, if what I hear is true."

Several heads in the group of anxious people were nodding, and glances slid away from my father with a kind of abashed hostility.

"Anyway, this was an accident, wasn't it?" Rik Gerson

said. He had brought his dinghy up to the slip and was
climbing out of it. He had collected up a lot of waterborne
detritus, as a good ecologist should, little of it connected
with the explosion of Freya's boat. His duck-boards were
covered with empty plastic bottles and pieces of poly-
styrene. There was a large roll of foam draught excluding
tape that he was absently wiping off with his sleeve. One
could see that the islanders did not much like him, Freya's
relation or no. Anona Aragon turned on him with her arms
classically akimbo.

"And so are you," she shouted. "An incomer. I saw you
last night sculling around and spying on us all." That
branch of the Aragons lived in a corrugated, rusty shack on
the water's edge. On the mainland it would never have been
permitted to be a human habitation. On the other hand, I
had heard Thetis Lisle say that those children were never
ill.

My father said, sounding very weak, "I am talking
about terrorism because I found this in my letters this
morning." He held up a square of card on which were three
black painted letters: F.L.F.

FAR FROM LEAVING HER COMPANIONS to cope with the emergency of Freya's death while she retreated into feminine hysterics, Tamara had hurried across The Hill to Trinder's Island. A girl who had seen two deaths by explosion could not believe that a third in her presence was accidental; and had not Freya told her that very morning about having overheard some cryptic, perhaps murderous, instructions to Nonie Anholt?

The dogs barked wildly when she approached The Castle, but nobody came out and Tamara went to hammer on the door. She did not know what she was looking for, but a surge of fury had not receded within her, and when her knock was unanswered she turned the handle and went in.

She looked through the ground-floor rooms, finding nobody. The place showed what its owner had made obvious, that she gloried in filth. Stalactites of cobweb dangled like something in a Hammer *House of Horror* movie, but the dirt was the prosaic, stinking gunge that any much-used, seldom-wiped kitchen would accumulate. Tamara had to go and gulp some fresh air before continuing her exploration. In what had been a dining-room there was an acrid smell, and the smears of oil on some otherwise relatively clean newspaper spread on the table made it look as though someone had been cleaning something there. Guns seemed more likely than shoes.

The stairs were made of imported wood, but the carvings on the banisters were hardly distinguishable from the dust that filled their interstices. The treads were dirty at the sides and smooth in the middle. Tamara went up, fastidiously not touching the greasy handrail.

Nonie Anholt had fallen, apparently some time before, and lay where she fell on what had once been a fur rug and was now a piece of beige, matted nastiness. Tamara thought that the massacre of the geriatrics had begun, first Freya, now Nonie, but as she moved closer, Nonie Anholt opened her crumpled eyes and said, "It's you. You're the girl that came the other day. What's your name?"

"Tamara Hoyland."

"I can't get up."

She was lying awkwardly, her arm at an unnatural angle under her. Tamara knelt down.

"Did you fall?"

"You keep asking such silly questions. Frank pushed me, of course."

Tamara's exotic training had included more than rudimentary first aid. She managed to turn and raise Mrs. Anholt, but it was clear that she had injured her leg as well as her wrist.

"You'll have to wait for me to fetch help."

"I realize that," the high voice said. A tough old bird, Tamara thought, and echoing her Mrs. Anholt said, "I am very tough. I dare say I'll break a hip and die of pneumonia in the accepted way, but not this time."

"I'll go and—"

"No, wait. I've lasted this long. I heard the explosion. Tell me—"

"There was an . . . accident. A boat—"

Nonie Anholt's mouth worked, and she seemed, oddly, to smile. "That's right. He promised me . . ." Her voice trailed away. After a while she said, "What I really want is a drink."

Swallow nothing before an anaesthetic; Tamara knew that. "You mustn't—"

"Just tea. Something hot."

"One isn't supposed to—"

"I did first aid too. Hot sweet tea."

"But if Thetis has to operate—"

"She can give me an emetic."

A special breed, the old women of Forway; Tamara wondered whether she would ever be as tough as Freya Barnes or Nonie Anholt. There was plenty of tea in the kitchen, for Irishmen had lived in this house. The milk was powder, though. Tamara stirred a good deal of the fly-spotted sugar into the dingy brew and carried it up. Nonie Anholt drank greedily.

"Make me pee, of course. Thetis Lisle will think I'm incontinent."

This was not the kind of establishment likely to contain a bedpan. "Do you want me to . . . ?"

"No. Just stay, don't leave me alone again." But her lids closed over those startling yellow eyes to show nothing but the mask of a pathetic old woman in need of succour. It took a long time to fetch it, even for a girl who could run all the way without collapsing on arrival at the quay. Selwyn Paull had fainted. Thetis Lisle was supervising his transfer to a stretcher, at the same time as keeping track over the landing of some peculiarly grisly jetsam from *The Pedro and Freya*. It was necessary to hurry, for the causeway would soon be covered. Thetis commandeered some men and John Yetts's Landrover, and they hurtled, if that is the word for an inevitably slowish journey, across the slimy stones.

Nonie Anholt recovered enough to act the *grande*

dame. "Thank you all so very much. So kind. I am so very much obliged . . ." until Thetis gave her a shot of some quick-acting sedative, and the undaunted voice trailed into silence.

As she watched the men manoeuvre the stretcher round the curve of the stairs, Tarmara found that she was fiddling with something in her jacket pocket and took out the coiled spring that she had removed from Freya Barnes's car two days before. It seemed a flimsy thing on which so much could depend. When she examined it closely, she saw scratches on the metal, and a shiny edge where the throttle spring had snapped across. It looked as though it had been filed almost to breaking point, so as to part whenever sudden pressure was exerted on it. Then Tamara also remembered the kinks she had seen in the brake pipe.

So Freya's death had been second time lucky, for someone—or third time; had not somebody mentioned that the suffering Sergeant Hicks had eaten a meal in Freya's house? Or fourth time lucky, or fifth? How could one tell what attempts had been made to dispose of Ian's mother before this last successful murder? It would have been just so easy to loosen the gas taps and fill the cabin with an explosive mixture that the chain-smoking, match-lighting Freya could not smell.

It would have been just as easy to spill transparent contact adhesive on Pedro Barnes's work-table; Tamara recalled to her memory what she had heard others say about the death of Ian's father. Tamara had been far away and had not been told, or enquired, the details at the time. Perhaps she had, in an undefined way, believed that Pedro died from grief. She knew the bare facts by now, for enough people on Forway were still chewing them over, all those months on, and it did not seem that there were more than bare facts to know. The explanation of a macabre accident had been universally accepted. Yet Tamara could imagine how easy it would had been for a visitor to spill the almost invisible liquid without Pedro noticing anything; and how easy, too, in such a storm, to bring down a power cable, leaving the laboratory hut to get gradually colder and colder.

Nonie's Irishman *would* have done it; of that Tamara was illogically, deplorably, sure. He could have done it, too. But why should he? Why should Frank, or whichever of his friends had been staying at Trinder's Castle a year before, have wished to wipe out the Barnes family?

Tamara sat on one of the filthy stairs, her head in her hands, fighting back nausea.

Always suspect coincidence. That had been one of her first lessons, both as an archaeologist and as a spy. And was it not the greatest coincidence of all to find that the three members of one nuclear family had all died unnatural deaths? Ian, Pedro, and now Freya . . . could there be one mind and one hand responsible?

Ian's car had been booby-trapped by terrorists. Although he had told Tamara that he was investigating drug importation at the time, she had assumed since that he must have been concealing from her his real assignment. She had never doubted since that day that the Irish terrorists were his target, as he had been theirs. But they could have had no conceivable interest in Ian's inoffensive parents.

Who could have wished for the extermination of the three members of the Barnes family? Who would benefit from those three deaths?

Means, opportunity, motive: Tamara had been taught that the last was the least significant.

Means? Available to anyone.

Opportunity: Who could have visited Pedro during the great gale? Who could have loosened a gas tap and in-

sulated a door on her boat? Who could have poisoned her
food?

John Yetts, who had serviced the van? Lena Gerson,
who brought Freya food? Or the discredited Selwyn Paull?

Selwyn Paull, whose telephone conversation overheard on that first day would admit of more than one
discreditable interpretation; who had claimed to check the
fan belt on the van for Freya; who could be sure not to eat
what he did not choose, as a guest in her house; Selwyn
Paull, who seemed to pull too many strings on Forway; who
would have known that Pedro would never support U.D.I.
but, having persuaded Pedro's widow otherwise, had the
greatest cause of anyone to dread the withdrawal of Freya
Barnes's material support.

Following the stretcher party back across the causeway
through the lapping tide, Tamara stood to one side as the
police Landrover bounced by, splashing up a wave of spray.
Two of the newly arrived security men were going to search
Trinder's Island and The Castle for subversives or explo-
sives. But the Irishman, Frank, and Dierdre Tyrone had
long since moved on from their refuge.

THE SCHOOLCHILDREN WERE DRAPING BUNTING in loops from the roof, little triangles of brightly coloured cloth against the stone. I was surprised to see a cardboard carton full of Union Jacks on sticks and equally surprised to find that all three shop windows displayed patriotic decorations. Mrs. Windows had put up a portrait of The Visitor, framed in a plait of red, white, and blue. My father was under sedation in Thetis Lisle's care and she said I should leave him in peace until the morning, so I set off to walk back to his house.

It was so rare to see Forway in this perfect calm and sun that I was touched by a charm to which I thought myself immune. The little patches of dank field scattered on the rough hillside, the smiling sea, even the heaps of drying turf, seemed full of some unique value that was worth preserving unaltered. But that was to sentimentalize. Tomorrow the wind would blow and the sea would roar; those shoots of corn would be stripped, that missing slate in a shed roof would be ripped into a gaping hole, salt would brown the petals of these rare orchids.

The two Yetts brothers were standing in a field now stripped of the cauliflower crop, bare stalks sticking unevenly above some healthy weeds.

"What next?" I asked casually.

"Not worth sowing anything now," John Yetts said.

"We'll be letting the land go," Fred said.

It was a small field, roughly five-sided, that hard toil had once won from the hillside. Its hedges were made of the stones removed from the ground, though there were many left, but by Forway standards it was not a bad patch. I did not know what he meant.

"Shan't be here much longer," Fred explained.

"Why not? You don't think the U.D.I. will work?"

"No chance."

"Why not?"

"It never was on, not really. Kind of play acting, wasn't it?"

"Have you thought that all along?"

The two brothers were very alike, long, angular men with dark brows. Put them in city suits or petunia robes and they would be naturals as peers or bishops. On Forway, in workmen's overalls, they did not look as sophisticated as they evidently were.

"We aren't soft, Magnus, just on account of being islanders."

"But you went along with it. I mean, you let people think—"

"Did you not hear about the money, then?" John Yetts said. "All Pedro Barnes's millions?"

"That's coming to the islanders, isn't it?" Fred agreed. "Equal shares between all Forway men and women resident for more than three years and aged over sixteen. That's the words, isn't it, John?"

They stood nodding identically. I was reminded of a cartoon in which the eyes are drawn as dollar signs. Had they been cheating Freya's generosity, I wondered? Or had she been bribing them to go along with her schemes?

"I thought the money was going into a trust," I said.

"Only if the Independence came off. Well, there wasn't any harm in her dreaming. Kept her and your dad really busy, these last months, making all their plans. Ever so happy, she was."

"Good way to go, really," Fred said.

John offered me a fill of tobacco, but I no longer smoke, so he lit his own pipe, and I watched him strike the match and remembered what happened to Freya when she did that last.

"I suppose it might have come off, all the same," Fred Yetts said. "If we hadn't heard all that about your dad, Magnus."

His brother replied derisively, "Don't be so daft, Freddie, how could it have? You wouldn't think the lad was in the navy and went to see the world, would you, Magnus? Just fancy being taken over by the Commies, do you, Fred? Wouldn't see much of Pedro Barnes's money then."

"Do any of the islanders think—?" I began.

"We was all playing along. All except Godfrey, that is. I'm not so sure about Thetis Lisle. Now Godfrey's a fine bloke, mind, nobody I'd sooner have in the lifeboat with me, but he isn't realistic. Bit of a dreamer, our Godfrey."

"What are you all going to do then?" I asked.

"We've put our share into a hotel in County Kerry, haven't we, Fred? Now the Windows, they've got an option on a ranch in Canada, and Annie Foggo's got plans on the mainland."

"You have all thought ahead, have you?"

"Damned fools if we hadn't. Way things are going, we'll all be off here come Michaelmas twelvemonth. Course, the old ones don't fancy the change much."

"You don't mind the idea of leaving Forway then?"

"Case of having to," Fred said.

"Can't stop progress, can you?" John said.

"My father thinks you can."

"Sure of that, are you?" John Yetts asked. "Or did he want to hand us over all nice and gift-wrapped to his foreign friends? There was a bloke called Hawker here the other day, said something that set us wondering. Could be your dad had some other plans than what he was telling us about."

"Now there's one who'll be the loser," Fred Yetts said, jerking his head at Rik Gerson's yellow van, which was bumping over the hillside towards us.

John Yetts did not try to conceal his satisfaction. "Not lived on the island three years, has he?"

"And he paid Peter Aragon well over the odds for that place."

"Compensation money, he said. From the Civil Service."

"Blessed if I can see why you can't be a civil servant with a bad memory," John remarked.

"Except that kind," his brother replied, gesturing at the men driving the police Landrover back to The Town. The island seemed to be swarming with them.

"Got to go through the motions, I suppose," John Yetts said, waving a casual hand to them. Rik Gerson pulled in beside us. He leaned out to say to me, "There you are. Someone has been trying to ring your father. He got on to me. Apparently your father's phone is bust."

"All right. Thanks." I left the Yetts brothers to their unprecedented and enjoyable idleness and went slowly onward.

There was no hurry. I left the track where a faint path turned downward towards a miniature plateau above the sea, known as Magnus's Splatt. It was here, nearly one hundred feet above the usual level of the sea, that a mariner from the wrecked *Thetis*, two days out of Liverpool, had been thrown by a mountainous wave, a piece of human flotsam, had survived the fearful injuries sustained from rocks and sea, to marry an island girl and beget an island son, and perpetuate another island name.

The episode would be unimaginable, on this calm and balmy day, to one who had not seen the fury of the elements against this Atlantic pimple. But I had been there on days when small boats were dashed to pieces in the harbour; when the Church roof was torn from its setting and the furniture within tossed out into the wind as though the wood were as insubstantial as balloons; when iron rails were twisted like wire in the storm. Sometimes the whole force of the Atlantic Ocean seems to concentrate on Forway, and the rock-laden surge sounds like the rumble of doom. No wonder, I thought, remembering that terrifying phenomenon, that the Yetts and the Windows and the other islanders are not sorry to leave. Given the hope of a share in the Barnes fortune with which to escape from this gaunt prison, I should not have been too scrupulous either.

MR. BLACK WAS CONSIDERABLY MORE INTERESTED in the news of Dierdre Tyrone and of Frank, presumably, he said, Hooley, than in Tamara's run-down of the events and atmosphere on Forway. She spoke to him at about the time that I was having the scales of illusion scraped from my eyes by the Yetts brothers, and of course, being what she was, Tamara already knew what I learned then. She had spent the evening in The Hotel with John Yetts, after the two of them had climbed down to rescue what they could from Freya's van, when I was stewing in a hospital bed. "I don't like whisky, especially with an *e* in it," Tamara told me, "but I drank it, and without water. They said the island was too short of that to waste it on spirits. But they told me what they were all really planning. Actually, what they were excited about was seeing The Visitor in the flesh. None of them gave a damn about politics. Just money and royalty."

Tamara was also forewarned about the accusations to be made about my father. Mr. Black read her the paragraph from an advance copy of the *Watchman*.

Mud sticks, and it is impossible to prove a negative. The defamatory statements were plausible. They were the kind of thing people enjoy believing. As I write, it is accepted by those who know, that the addition of the name of

Selwyn Paull to that demonology of establishment traitors is unjustified, yet once named, never believed innocent.

He is, however, innocent of that charge. The Prime Minister has affirmed so in The House of Commons; his former colleagues have supported him in letters and interviews. Tamara Hoyland, who had cause to wonder, is now certain, as I am, that he was no more than he claimed: a retired administrator of limited imagination, who was guilty of nothing more reprehensible than bad judgement.

Circumstances had conspired against him. Carl Hawker's accusation had fallen into ground made fertile by suspicion. It could all have been true.

Tamara and I were not the only people who had heard him, at various moments, discussing the progress of the independence plans on the telephone, but even that was harmless, not, as I had feared, a progress report to a foreign master. I found the explanation in his papers, once it was obvious that he would never return to sort them out himself. Tamara had found it some time before. She searched through them on the evening of Freya's death, the evening before The Visit.

I had not gone back to my father's house before a late and drunken bedtime. But the persistent telephone caller tracked me down. Lena Gerson, like the Ancient Mariner, had called me in to tell me how dreadful Freya's death had been.

"I have never known anyone that died like that before." Unanswerable; who had?

"You will miss her, I expect," I said. I realized that I would miss her too. Having lost my own mother when I was twelve, I had always been kindly treated by Freya on my visits to Forway, and it was she who interceded for me when my father was in one of his frequent furies about my imperfections. He would have preferred a son like Ian, who was good at everything physical. My father and Ian had often gone off together to shoot or fish, while I stayed with Freya to talk about poetry or listen to her stories of life in a university town. I am not pretending that she was ever like a mother to me; only that I felt suddenly bereaved.

Lena Gerson's house was in a mess. Some half-spun wool was smouldering with a horrible stink on the hearth. Through the open door into the lean-to kitchen, I could see an open, half-packed suitcase.

"Are you going away?" I asked the question out of purely social politeness, but she looked terrified and denied it so vehemently that I began to think about it. Why were the Gersons packing up? Surely those who had chosen to abandon civilization for Forway should be among the last to leave it again? In any case, the day of forced evacuation must still be far off. They could have months more of the Good Life.

She, and I, were distracted by her telephone. "It's the same man, he's been ringing and ringing to reach your father," she said. "He said he'd been given our number for emergencies." What did I expect? A guttural Eastern European voice issuing commands? A sinister Chinese one demanding explanations?

It was my godfather, Philip Cooper, my father's old friend from Cambridge days. They had taken the same exams, chosen the same career, and for forty years corresponded across the world about the problems of maintaining British rule across the seas. Now Philip Cooper lived in mourning for the beautiful territory over which he had once presided. He was racked with guilt that he had assented to its dismemberment. When he stood there in plumes and sword beside Princess Margaret and watched the Union Flag lowered for the last time, he had felt, he told me once, as though he should draw that sword from its scabbard and impale himself upon it. I think he always remained ashamed that he had survived that day. He lived in a bungalow near Eastbourne and in his genteel comfort read about anarchy in the land he had cherished.

The vultures had not smelt Philip Cooper out yet; he was not ringing about Carl Hawker. He wanted to know whether my father had remembered to notify the Holy See at Rome in his preparations for Independence.

"So many things to think about, my boy, and nobody else to do the staff work," Philip told me. "It will be a miracle if we manage without any omissions. Have to get the formalities right. Of the utmost importance."

"I will tell him. Have you been in on this from the beginning?"

"Right from the start. A heaven-sent chance to put one thing right before I pass on, you might say."

There was a fat file of correspondence between the two men. When I read the letters from Philip Cooper and the carbons of my father's replies, I was reminded of two gleeful schoolboys on a spree, the last fling of a pair of superannuated men of the world.

"Mind you mention the Vatican to him, Magnus. It is these little details that make all the difference."

I left Lena Gerson to her secretive clearing up. I couldn't blame her if she was planning to leave the wretched Rik, now that Freya was not there to need her ministrations.

Outside their shack, the hole in which the Gersons flung their trash, obtrusively close to my father's windows, was overflowing. They ate a lot of tinned food. I kicked some loose gash towards the heap and noticed among it a square-cornered tin, about the size of one of John Yetts's tobacco tins, which was labelled "Fuses from ICI."

It will be obvious by now that I am a man of inaction

and have led a protected life. I merely wondered why the Gersons should have needed fuses, in a dwelling that had not even self-generated electricity, and then I assumed that my father had thrown the tin there when he discarded it. The electrical fuses frequently need replacing, with the fluctuating supply provided by a wind generator. The word meant nothing else to me. But it did to Tamara, and she heard me mention it later, when I was making some joke about the self-sufficient Gersons' diet. To her, fuses were not necessarily connected with heating or lighting.

WHEN TAMARA ENTERED SELWYN PAULL'S HOUSE later
that evening, she was safe from intrusion because his son
was drunk in The Hotel. She drew the curtains (crimson
velvet, lined and inter-lined) to prevent any chinks of light
falling into the yard that separated that house from the Gersons', and she went through all Selwyn Paull's possessions
and papers. She was methodical, and so had he been, so
that it did not take her too long. The filing cabinet,
unlocked, contained the recorded history of a civil servant's
life, divided into brown folders: certificates, licences, poli-
cies, testaments, and reports. Numerous letters had been
preserved and filed under the correspondent's name: his
wife, his son, his parents, his colleagues. The arrangements
for Forway's independence were neatly documented and
discussed at length in the file of correspondence from Philip
Cooper. By the time she had finished her investigation in
the house, Tamara did not believe that Selwyn Paull was
anything but what he seemed and what he claimed to be.

Tamara's contact "in the know" was Thea Crawford's
husband, Sylvester. She rang him from Freya's house to ask
about Carl Hawker. He made the noise that goes with coming across a nauseating smell.

"What's wrong with him, Sylvester?"

"To be pompous, it's a question of professional ethics."

Crawford himself worked for a paper that was both puritan
and highbrow and often pompous. "If you accept that my
job is a profession at all."

"Do you mean that he doesn't protect his informants?"

"The opposite, in a way. He's a smears man. He has
sold out. A young man on the make. Haven't you ever noticed how convenient his exposures can be for the establishment? What was the one a few weeks ago . . . that man
who sneaked to his MP about contracts at the weapons fac-
tory, the one Hawker claimed was in the pay of the East
Germans?"

"But it all turned out to be nonsense."

"There was no evidence or corroboration, if that's what
you mean. But the man killed himself all the same. It's the
proverbial situation. Mud sticks. No smoke without a fire.
Our masters find it convenient to have a supposedly independent journalist who is prepared to discredit people who
are inconvenient. Even if the allegations could be proved to
be untrue, which is impossible by definition, it would be too
late."

"But, Sylvester. If this is known about Hawker, why
does anyone believe him? Or publish his articles?"

"Because it is sometimes true. Just occasionally. He has
had one or two genuine scoops in his time. Anyway, his stories sell papers."

Tamara hung the receiver up very thoughtfully. What
a neat arrangement, she thought, and how characteristic of
the Mr. Black she was beginning to understand, a man for
whom all was fair in his war. No wonder he had not been
especially interested in her reports from Forway once Tamara had confirmed what he needed to know, the identity
of the moving spirit of the independence movement. Carl
Hawker's story would bring the islanders to their senses.
Once they heard it, and some had already heard it, they

would be convinced that Selwyn Paull was leading them by the nose to the slaughterhouse; that he was not interested in their well-being but that of the Russian Paymasters for whom he had worked throughout his career. They would visualize the course of events with horrible clarity; independence, followed by conquest—and being turned into a base for attacks on a country to which they all, in fact, felt loyal.

Carl Hawker was onto a good thing; the secret hatchet man, out there in the public eye, popular on TV, handsomely paid, and all the richer for his tax-free extras; a corrupted whizz kid.

Helping herself to some food in the kitchen, which already felt bleak from the withdrawal of the personality that had pervaded it, Tamara considered the pattern of Mr. Black's operation on Forway and wondered whether he had followed a similar one earlier in the year. When he chose Tamara to worm her way into the confidence of Mike and Rory, telling her to report on their plans, identify their allies, and eventually make it possible for them to be arrested red-handed, had he planned, had he intended, that neither of the two men would survive his association with Tamara Hoyland? When he read those psychologists' reports and aptitude-test results about Tamara, had he recognized a woman who would take her own violent action? Had he seen in Tamara what some other unscrupulous man had seen in Dierdre Tyrone?

Tamara's satisfaction in revenge was tarnished by the thought that some other mind than hers might have planned it. She hated to think that a motivated human could be turned into a lethal weapon, manipulated in a third party's cause. Had she been as cynically deceived as the indignant public cheated into detestation of Selwyn Paull? Were "freedom fighters" moulded into spearheads by a totalitarian power? Did even the murderous Irish, su-

preme in Tamara's demonology, attack people who were the
enemies of people unconnected with their own interests?
Many unpublished grudges must be wiped out under a false
banner of political action.

When she had joined Mr. Black's team, her motives
had been simple—revenge; and she had believed that his
was, if different, equally simple: the good of his country.
Her mental model of the world had been as simple as a
child's drawing of a house, flat, symmetrical, with nothing
behind it, the good guys and the baddies, right and wrong,
expiation and revenge. But things are not so simple. Mr.
Black's intentions were probably as devious as his methods.
An analogy: a billiard-table. Tamara saw herself as a ball,
edged from one angle to move at a different one, with a
skilful player calculating the geometry. So, if he had expected her disobedient initiative, when he turned her atten-
tions to Rory and Mike, what had he expected her to do on
Forway? More, surely, than report back to him by telephone. He had not needed Tamara's presence on the island
to arrange Carl Hawker's visit. What was she here for? Why
had he sent her to a place where Ian would be so clearly in
her mind? Did he know that she would be shaken by surges
of punitive fury whenever she thought of him in the setting
where she had been with him before? If she was Mr. Black's
weapon, whether bludgeon or rapier, at whom was she
aimed?

FRIDAY MORNING. The Day. The day of The Visit, of Independence, the day before which numbers had been crossed off on calendars; a rather different day from that which I had heard presaged by my father and the Lisles and Freya Barnes. There was an atmosphere of "last times" on Forway; of repairs not worth making, seeds not worth planting, resources not worth saving.

Dawn—and the moaning of the fog-horn. The brilliant warmth of the previous day was followed by an impenetrable haze. The ferry from Cornwall edged its way through the fog to deliver its load of passengers and papers and was away again by eight o'clock. The captain said that visibility was worsening. The Visitor was due to arrive later in the day by helicopter, one of those twenty-four seaters with room for the attendant crew of pressmen and photographers. But the helicopter was subject to the rules of the Civil Aviation Authority. No passenger transport was permitted to try to land with less than nine hundred metres of visibility.

I felt my way down to The Town like a blind man, for I left the path several times and was afraid of walking over the cliff edge. By my own reckoning, visibility was not even one metre. I knew I was in The Town from the sound of Jeannie Windows's professionally cheery voice assuring the schoolchildren that the weather would clear and The Visitor would come. "Come along, children, let's get on with it. What about some flags for this corner here?" I wondered whether the children could even see the corner. We should not have been surprised by the fog. It often followed a warm day on Forway.

I was on my way to see my father. Thetis Lisle had told me that he had suffered a very mild stroke and that I should not worry, so I turned into The Hotel first. Annie Foggo looked embarrassed when she saw me. She was growing rich out of my persecutors. The ferry had brought a cargo of newsmen, who surged towards me with questions about my father.

I parried their attacks with my back to the bar. They grew bored after a while, for I knew one or two of them, and Annie Foggo had already told them that I had very seldom come to the island since my father lived there. Some of the talk was about the oil, for there had apparently been a press release, embargoed until today. The Visitor was going to announce the plans my father and Freya had feared, later in the day.

Fortified by alcohol, I went out again into the mist. It was not like town fog, it did not choke one's throat and blacken everything one touched, but wisps of it crept into houses, and even in the bar wafted between me and my interrogators, lending an unreal air to the atmosphere. But then, I had never really thought that Forway was part of the quotidian world.

My father was doped still but had been talking restlessly in his unconsciousness, Thetis told me. Nonie Anholt was in the other bed.

"I haven't been so busy for years," Thetis whispered. She was in her doctor's rig, with a white coat on, and a stethoscope hanging on her bosom. She looked competent and severe and bustled out of the room with that air of busy preoccupation that medical students learn along with anatomy.

My father was snoring now, hoarse breaths blowing the wisps of his moustache up and down in the still air. But Nonie Anholt was tossing around uncomfortably, and across the passage, Thetty Yetts, now in labour, was making the noises associated by bachelors like me with the steamier television dramas.

Nonie Anholt opened her cats' eyes and stared straight at me. "What was he saying?" she said in her clear Knightsbridge voice. "What did he say about Freya Barnes?"

I did not think I should reply. Surely delirious old women should be protected from such news. But she was at least temporarily *compos mentis* and pressed me, so that I found myself telling her of Freya's dreadful death. She said, "That's not right. Not Freya. He promised me . . ." Her voice died away. I waited uneasily. There was no role for me in this macabre sick bay, but through the half-open door I could see that Thetis Lisle and her assistant, Jeannie Foggo, were fully occupied, and the crescendoes of sound from Thetty Yetts inhibited me from interrupting their hard labour. It was not an amusing pun, I told myself severely, as an egalitarian man should; but it did seem apt.

The morning wore on. The fog was not lifting at all.

Nonie Anholt began to speak, rapidly and wildly. With clumsy hands I tried to smooth her sheets and plump her pillows, the useless actions that I supposed proper nurses would perform, but she spoke on, and after a while I was able to gather what she was trying to tell—not me, but anyone who could hear.

"I said I'd show them, I'd show the Brits, I'd pay them out . . ."

There is no point in my trying to reproduce her words

verbatim, for she was very incoherent and repetitive, and it was a long while before I understood what she was saying. It was this: that she had given Frank refuge, and Dierdre Tyrone, and others of their fellow revolutionaries before them, in the hope of helping to punish the Brits, as she referred to them. The Brits had caused the death of her young lover. I remembered the papers in the island Log and realized what she was talking about. I also remembered that she must have been both married to someone else and widowed by the time the young man was killed "while trying to escape." But she had never forgiven the British for his death and had been planning revenge ever since.

I had time, as she repeated herself, to wonder how true her words were. What I had heard of her London life did not sound like that of a bitter woman driven by unappeasable rancour. Presumably she had revived her anger once she returned to live on Forway.

Frank and Dierdre had made plans, too. They had promised Nonie Anholt that they would do something drastic to "show the Brits." She regarded it partly as payment for her taking them in, though Frank had been her lover. I found that a peculiarly revolting thought. Their target was to be The Visitor. The Visitor would be a suitable target and deserved to suffer for the United Kingdom's crimes. But not Freya Barnes. That was why Nonie was so agitated now. Freya Barnes was not a proper victim.

Dierdre and Frank had promised they would not hurt anyone on the island. Only property and The Visitor. But Nonie Anholt said, more than once, that they had not been the cause of the explosion at the Coastguard Station. That was someone else. They were angry. They didn't like other people doing that on their patch. Nonie had been jealous. "I wanted one for Nonie," she said several times, the child she had been surfacing in the aged carapace. "One for Nonie. A blow against the Brits. He said he'd do it for me."

But Freya Barnes should not have suffered. They had promised. This went on and on, and then on again. It felt like hours. At last Thetis came in and shot something into the old woman's arm, so that she fell silent and her eyes closed. Thetis told me briskly that there was nothing I could do for my father mooning around here, and returned to her other patient.

Outside in The Square, the day was still muffled by fog. The usual sounds of Forway were indistinct murmurs, the very smell was damped down. But I could hear loud wails from the school.

I bumped into Rik Gerson on my way across The Square and then came upon Tamara standing outside The Hotel. I said something idle about Rik Gerson, remarking that the weather he had seen when he came over prospecting a year ago should have put him off Forway for good.

"I didn't know he'd been here then," she said a little sharply. "You mean he was here on the island when Pedro Barnes died?"

"That's right. I thought you knew. And now poor old Freya. Do you think that was an accident, Tamara? Listen to what Nonie Anholt has been rambling on about."

I told her all that Nonie had been saying.

TAMARA HAD THE TELEPHONE RECEIVER IN HER HAND and was beginning to dial Mr. Black's number again, when she heard a sound from her room, Ian's former bedroom. Rik Gerson was standing there, holding the miniature camera which she had not had occasion to use on this mission.

"Neat little thing," he said. "In my day they looked like cigarette lighters."

"Smoking is so unfashionable these days." Tamara watched him return the gadget to the tampon box and push the drawer closed. He held his finger and thumb together.

"Want me to stick the hair back again?"

"Please don't bother."

"I thought you must be one of Mr. Black's army."

"Did you?"

"Funny coincidence, really." He walked past her into the living-room. "Okay if I take a drink?" He poured one for himself. "I mean, two of the chaps working in Department E having connections with this place."

"Did you meet Lena through working with Ian?"

"Yeah."

"Ian never mentioned you to me."

"He wasn't supposed to mention his work to you at all."

"Didn't Lena know what you did?"

"You kidding? She would have told half London."

"Do you still work for Department E?" Tamara asked.

"No."

"But you sent Mr. Black one of the U.D.I. leaflets."

"For old times' sake," Rik Gerson said.

"Or to make sure that Forway wouldn't drain away the Barnes fortune?"

"Once a member of Mr. Black's team, always a member."

"You put your heart into it, did you?" Tamara said savagely. He did not seem to understand her. He replied, "It was a job, of course, not a crusade."

"Why did you stop?"

"I was invalided out."

"What had happened to you?"

"I had a knock on the head and it made my memory wonky. And my sense of balance."

"That sounds easy to fake."

"But it all turned out very nicely for me in the end. It's not as though I was ever exactly dedicated to it as a career. I got a very decent little pay-off."

"Insurance on special Civil Service terms," Tamara quoted.

"That's how we paid for the Aragons' place."

"It seemed like a good idea to live near the rich widow, did it?" Tamara said. "Once she'd been made into a widow."

"That's right. Lena's her only relation. Infertile lot, that family, I'm glad to say."

"With one blood relation left to inherit." Tamara went over to Freya's desk and took from it the envelope that had arrived the previous day in the mail. She extracted its contents.

Tamara unfolded the stiff paper. It was typed in those very large letters used for legal documents, with wide margins, but even London lawyers could not much complicate

the deed's simple provisions. There were only three para-
graphs. Tamara picked up the pen that Freya always used
and tested that its ink was flowing. Then she wrote the
name Freya Barnes, in Freya's handwriting, in the space beside which a cross had been pencilled.

"You can be one of the witnesses," she said. She wrote
her own name, Tamara Hoyland, her address in London,
and her profession, archaeologist.

She held the pen out to Rik Gerson. She warned him,
"No spoilt papers, mind."

He looked at her with what seemed like admiration. "A
gutsy lady," he said. "And a good try. Who'd have thought
that the plight of the islanders would have grabbed you like
that? But no way, no way at all. That money is going to
make the Gerson family very happy."

"I have no idea what the criminal laws of Forway
would have been if it had become an independent state,"
Tamara said. "They might have started from scratch. You
might have been allowed to get away with murder. You
might even have been able to profit from a murder you
committed. But so long as you remain a citizen of the
United Kingdom, a murder or manslaughter committed by
you can be tried in England. That's in the British Nation-
ality Act. So it won't make any difference if Forway turns
out to be French or Irish or even nothing at all. You are still
British and you can be tried in England for the murder of
Freya Barnes. Let alone the murder of Pedro, a year before."

She had been prepared for Rik Gerson to attack her.
But his training had been as extensive as hers. He said
calmly, "Proof?"

"Has been created."

"By you?"

"Who else?"

"Unwise."

"The mailboat took its details," Tamara said. "I dare say you were a better pupil of that brutal trainer in Bayswater than I ever was, but proving it would not help you now. In fact, keeping me safe and well is extremely important to you."

"That's an old trick."

"None the worse."

"There's no way of proving what was done to that boat. There's nothing left of it or the gas cylinder. Quite apart from the fact that you can't blame me if she lit a match in her own cabin."

"One of your tools was found in the wreck of the Bedford van," Tamara told him. "Your fingerprints were on it."

"That is not true. I didn't—"

"And you can't prove that. The tool's on its way to the mainland."

"That doesn't mean a thing," Gerson said.

"And you left the rope from your dinghy tied to the rail of Freya's boat that night. Humphrey Lisle unhitched it when he rowed her out there. I found it in his boat."

"You can't identify rope."

"You can when it's entangled with homespun wool."

"You have framed me," he said; his face was vicious.

"No, just forged your signature. That's my specialty."

He turned the trust deed over in his hands and re-read a paragraph; then he said, "Anything else?"

"I dare say I could show that you fixed the explosion at the Coastguard Station, if necessary. You'd been so desperate to stop Freya's plans going through. Don't forget, I've been taught how to create instability too."

He rubbed thoughtfully at the bald patch on his head. Tamara said slowly, "When was it exactly that you were wounded on the head so conveniently?"

"Spring, last year."

"Ian died then."

"That's right."

Tamara stared at the man. He looked like the victim of
a deprived urban childhood, rather small and too thin. Her
trained eye observed the balance of his body though, the
ever-readiness of his reactions. The pair of them were
equally well disguised. She said, "You were the man they
said was with Ian when he died. That's when you were injured. 'Incapacitated for work though not for ordinary life,'
those were Mr. Black's words."

"So?"

"What happened? Why weren't you in the car? If it
blew up as they said, you couldn't have escaped so lightly."

"It was when he started the engine. I was not in the car
yet. I was hit by flying debris."

"Was he killed at once?"

"So they said."

"And you were unconscious?"

"Yes."

"So when did you take his gold pencil? A souvenir, was
it? A reminder of a narrow escape? A tip from the terrorists? A thank-you present for fingering Ian to them? Your
thirty pieces of silver?"

"What do you mean?"

"You were out of range, somewhere safe. You weren't
unconscious. Not then. I dare say they knocked you out con-
vincingly enough. You saw Ian after that explosion. Answer
me now. Did he die at once?"

"Well, almost."

Tamara launched herself at the man, her reactions
speeded but her judgement dimmed by the intensity of her
revengeful fury.

DOWN IN THE TOWN, I had eventually braved the bar again and, fortified by the last of the brandy ("The drink's nearly run out with this lot here," Annie Foggo warned), had said more than I meant to the gathered newshounds. Local people popped in and out to say that the fog was, or was not, lifting. When the door opened, letting in more wisps of white nothingness, ever-louder noises could be heard from the school, where presumably the children blamed their elders for the weather. Their elders blamed fate.

The journalists had moved on from my father in particular to the moving spirits behind U.D.I. in general. We all moved on from whisky to rum.

Eleven o'clock, eleven-thirty, midday . . . the fog remained as earth-bound as the sea itself.

At half-past twelve the final definitive message was relayed around The Town. The Visitor's helicopter would not take off. The Visit was cancelled.

The other visitors were much put out. No booze, no story, no escape . . . I was far from sober. I said, "Come on, then, if that's what you're interested in. I'll show you all the Independence papers."

Shambling, but not straggling so far as to lose sight of my lurching figure, they followed me up the hill through the fog. If I had been soberer, I should have worried about these erratic strangers falling off Forway in the engulfing mist, but they say that drunkards don't fall and these did not, although by the time we had panted up to the Barnes place, several had collapsed, and only three of the men were still with me. I registered but did not recognize the heaving, grunting noise I heard when I opened the door. I called, "Anyone here?"

The door into the living-room was flung open. Rik Gerson stood there, panting. Blood was running from his nose and from a gash on the side of his neck. He was bent over, one hand cradling his genitals. We stood aside stupidly, as he pushed by and out of the house.

Tamara Hoyland was in the sitting-room. She was getting up slowly from the floor. All but the heaviest pieces of furniture were overturned or askew. I tripped over a reel of cotton. Freya's work-table had fallen over and open. Tamara held a pair of dressmakers' scissors at an aggressive angle. Her cheek was bruised. When she put her weight on her right foot, she winced and sat down on the upended armchair.

"I kicked him too hard," she said and rubbed her foot. Her cheeks were scarlet, her eyes shining. Like me, the journalists gazed at her with delight.

One of them said, "What on earth's been going on?" And another answered, "I should have thought that's obvious."

"Are you all right, Tamara?" I said.

"Never better," she assured me, her eyes glistening.

"Did he try . . ." I began.

"It was nothing," she said. "Just between the two of us."

One of the journalists began to pick up the things that were scattered around the room. From where she sat, Tamara reached out for a stiff piece of paper, some sort of document, and casually folded it up and put it into her pocket.

"I came to show these people the documents that were prepared for Forway's U.D.I.," I explained. Tamara smiled brilliantly at the journalists.

"Would a bit later do?" she said. "Let me clear up first."

"We'll help you."

"No, no, I can manage." With remarkable speed, considering the stubbornness alcohol usually induces, she persuaded them to leave now and come back later. I realized that they were only so docile because they hoped to get a better story from Rik Gerson. I refused to depart with them, but when they had gone, Tamara said, "If you're staying anyway, Magnus, make yourself useful. I could do with some coffee."

"Tamara . . . are you sure that Rik didn't . . . ?"

"You can see for yourself," she said. Her sleeve was torn, but her jeans undamaged, it was true.

"You are obviously able to defend yourself." I am not sure whether I sounded admiring, approving, or envious.

She laughed and said, "I've learned some judo, that's all. Anyway, you broke it up almost before it had started."

While I was getting out cups and coffee, I heard the telephone bell tinkle nine times; she was apparently ringing someone in London. Tamara's voice was raised, but I could not hear her words through the closed kitchen and bedroom doors. When she came through to the kitchen, she had changed her jersey, and combed her hair, and looked like a nymph instead of a maenad. When she had drunk some coffee, into which I had poured some of Freya's brandy, she pulled the legal document from her pocket.

"I thought you might fill this in," she said. I took it from her. It was the trust deed in which Freya made over the Barnes fortune to the people of Forway. Tamara had witnessed her signature. I looked doubtfully at the blank space.

"One's supposed to see the person actually signing," I said dubiously.

"You'd rather that Rik Gerson and his wife get it all?"

I took the pen from her and wrote my name underneath Tamara's and Freya's signatures.

THE ROLE OF DR. WATSON, when Sherlock Holmes is played by a youngish woman, is not a flattering one. I am aware that I come out of this story seeming an ass. Nor is my appearance in that guise deceptive, although appearances so often are. This narrative, for instance, may have seemed to be a political thriller. It turns out to be an old-fashioned story of murder and detection. One thing, however, has gone according to the formula. The ninny with whom the detective shares the clues, and from whom the detective hears of them, falls in love with the detective. Tamara Hoyland is a permanent inhabitant of my heart and mind. She's amusing herself with me, using me as her reward. I keep hoping for more. She may learn to love me. But like the heroes of fiction, she seems intent on moving forward to her next assignment without me. She has been very kind. She has talked to me about that week on Forway in the most patient and indulgent manner. She has explained all that I did not understand and made me privy to conversations that she did not understand. She has given me information that she should not have passed: for instance, that Frank Hooley and Dierdre Tyrone, alias Emma Hurst, were arrested when they slipped ashore from a fishing boat somewhere near Falmouth and that they credibly denied any intention of harming The Visitor to Forway. "It would have been suicide," the man is said to have exclaimed. "No kamikaze missions for us." Like Freya Barnes, Nonie had been cheated in her attempt to make a final impression on the world. Dierdre Tyrone was returned to the Irish Republic to complete her term of imprisonment there. Tamara was astonished to find pity in her own reaction to this news. She had the feeling that the girl had been drawn into something that she never quite understood and later regretted. Hooley is still awaiting trial on charges of murder alleged to have been committed in Birmingham two years ago.

I wanted to know whether she would ever have left Rik Gerson at liberty, to use on any other inconvenient victim the skills that he had learned from the same instructor as herself. Could she have let the murderer of Ian Barnes and both his parents go free?

"That was how I first realized he must have worked for Department E, actually," she told me. "When his wife used a phrase the instructor uses. A spot of turbulence—that's what that man would call the third world war. And those references to a special Civil Service insurance, too."

"Anyone who had received your training would know how to blow up something much more challenging than a disused coastguard station," I said, nuzzling my face into that soft patch between throat and collar-bone. Tamara was not just being kind. She enjoyed it as much as I did, probably more; for my distracted emotions came between me and abandonment.

"You wouldn't need any training to know how to undo a gas tap and insulate a door," she said. "Even you could have done it, Magnus."

"I doubt if I could have done the other thing. I don't know anything about the inside of cars."

"I don't know that Rik Gerson did either. I showed that

throttle spring to a mate of mine in London, and he said it would have looked just the same if it had suddenly snapped from old age."

"What about the brake line, though?"

"Who knows? A lot can happen in a two-hundred-foot fall."

"Would you have used that evidence you manufactured?"

"I should never have been allowed to. Think of the beans he might have spilt if he got in a witness-box."

Tamara had got answers from Mr. Black in the end—perhaps not true, but convincing. Ian had not been on an Irish assignment. His death at terrorist hands had been an unexplained surprise to Department E. Now, however, it was clear that Gerson had betrayed him in the hope that he would be murdered—the first step on a journey towards a dazzling inheritance.

"I hope he's frying in hell," she said uncharacteristically.

"On earth he's a hero instead."

In that blinding fog on the day of The Visit, a ship had gone onto Forway's barrier of rocks. It had radioed for help. Without the distorting fog, they could have been seen and heard quite easily. As it was, there was a nightmarish scene that should be described by a more vivid pen than mine. I'd got down to The Town by then. I was looking for Rik Gerson. I almost thought I might kill him.

All the men then in The Town had rushed towards the lifeboat slip, myself inevitably with them. John Yetts was the coxswain. He said, "Not you, Magnus, you're no good in boats."

Rik Gerson climbed in unchallenged, and the lifeboat disappeared from our sight almost the moment it was cast off.

"There's no danger," the women said. "It's glassy calm." There should have been no danger. Rik Gerson need not have stood on the gunwale to help a swimming mariner into the boat; Rik should have been tied on, as the rules required, and all the others were. When he fell into the sea, he disappeared from view. Nobody saw him surface, nor could he be found in the fog, although the lifeboat stayed out looking for him for hours. He could not have survived, although sometimes Tamara has nightmares in which he did, and lives in comfort with Ian Barnes unavenged.

It was a hero's death and Rik's wife Lena has been presented with a medal by the Royal Humane Society. I doubt, though, that it consoled her for the loss of Freya Barnes's fortune. She is said to have taken the government compensation for the Aragons' place without disputing the very low figure set on property values in Forway by the official valuer, and we hear that she has gone back to being a secretary in London. No doubt she now spends her lunch-hours gazing into the windows of the shops from which she had expected to buy her clothes with the Barnes millions. Since she loved secretarial work, as she had said, she is probably happy.

The dead Gerson and the living one, in fact, were more fortunate than my innocent father. He never recovered from Mr. Black's exercise in technique. He suffered a second stroke while he was still in Thetis Lisle's care, and now he is paralyzed and incontinent and lives in a geriatric hospital in West London. If the staff are whispering that he was once a traitor and a spy, he cannot understand them. Perhaps I should say that he has no way of indicating it, if he does.

Tamara and I do not live together. I want more than that and have less. I long to marry her, to exchange mutual promises of perpetual fidelity, to feel that she is mine. I know it is old-fashioned; but once you feel about a girl as I do about Tamara, you realize that any previous conviction of love has been counterfeit.

Tamara will not even let me spend the night in her flat. She has entertained me there to decorous meals, but she will only lie with me in my bed. The impermanence makes me restless, for she will not stay for long or leave her belongings there, and she keeps rushing off to get on with her backlog of work at the Royal Commission. Soon she will leave me permanently behind her. I am no more than light physical relief—the biter bit.

Even on Saturdays and Sundays she sets the alarm clock too early. But I am physically stronger and can hold her to me.

"How did you know it was Rik, anyway?" I said.

"I am ashamed to admit." She pushed me away with a trained twist of the torso and stood up, a heavenly sight in the most literal sense of the words. "I just knew. The evidence was all there, all the indications were quite definite. All the things you told me you had see—"

"I didn't know they meant anything."

"The ICI fuse tin in the midden. The insulating tape in his dinghy. Anona Aragon seeing him rowing around that evening. And they had such a massive motive for killing Freya before she completed the trust deed. Then it seemed to me so obvious that they were faking about their simple-lifery. Lena was pining for Piccadilly. Worth being away from it to her, of course; she thought there were millions involved."

Once the various taxes had been deducted, according to the laws of the United Kingdom, there was less money than expected, but still enough to make each Forway family prosperous when it was shared out between them.

I went there in the following spring. I had been com-

missioned to write a piece called "The Last Days of Forway" for a Sunday colour supplement.

The Yetts family had already left, with the baby whose
name had been changed from Independence to Elizabeth.
Annie Foggo had married a publican from Plymouth but
come back to Forway for the occasion. All the others were
sticking it out to the end, though they knew it was only for
a few months more. Even the Lisles had made their plan.
Thetis was going into partnership with a general practi-
tioner in the Outer Hebrides.

The three governments that claimed the rights to Forway had agreed that whichever of them was adjudged its
historical owner at the International Court would facilitate
the completion of the oil rig and terminal, so that the only
dispute, like all disputes are in the end, was about money.

Meanwhile, at the second attempt, the first and last
Royal Visit was to take place. I was standing in the Press
pound in The Square on Forway when the Royal Yacht
anchored in the island's waters. The islanders cheered continuously as the launch was lowered, the Visitor descended
to it, and the pipes shrilled. There were tears in most eyes,
even my own, when those feet touched the pier, and there
arose to the top of the newly erected flagpole that brightly
coloured scrap of fabric, the Union Flag.